"I'm Going To Win This Case, Get Married And Run For Office. That's The Plan."

"Plans can change, but only if you want them to."

He regarded her for several seconds, and Maggie was afraid she'd crossed some line. "What I want is to do the right thing. I always do."

What was the "right" thing here? Was it right to like him? To want him to like her? To imagine what it would be like to kiss him? Was it right to want to see him again—without testimony or lawyers, without messy histories or future campaigns involved?

Was it right to want those things without any other expectations?

Dear Reader,

When last we saw James Carlson, he arrested the bad guy and saved the day. Many readers wondered whether or not James would ever meet his match. Have no fear— *A Man of Privilege* answers that question!

James is a wealthy man with a spotless record. He's destined for higher office and the power that goes with it. All goes according to plan until Maggie Eagle Heart walks into his life. He's completely unprepared for the beautiful woman who challenges him at every turn. No one has ever challenged him before. Maggie is different— and it won't be long until James discovers just how different she really is!

James finds himself struggling to keep his family's expectations and his own dreams spinning when Maggie is around. Before he knows it, things spin out of control.

A Man of Privilege is a sexy story of power and privilege. I hope you enjoy reading it as much as I enjoyed writing it! Be sure to stop by www.sarahmanderson.com for a sneak peek at the next book, *A Man of Distinction.*

Sarah

SARAH M. ANDERSON

A MAN OF PRIVILEGE

HARLEQUIN®

entertain, enrich, inspire™

ISBN-13: 978-0-373-73184-8

A MAN OF PRIVILEGE

Books by Sarah M. Anderson

Harlequin Desire

A Man of His Word #2130
A Man of Privilege #2171

SARAH M. ANDERSON

Award-winning author Sarah M. Anderson may live east of the Mississippi River, but her heart lies out west on the Great Plains. With a lifelong love of horses and two history teachers for parents, she had plenty of encouragement to learn everything she could about the tribes of the Great Plains.

When she started writing, it wasn't long before her characters found themselves out in South Dakota among the Lakota Sioux. She loves to put people from two different worlds into new situations and see how their backgrounds and cultures take them someplace they never thought they'd go.

When not helping out at school or walking her two rescue dogs, Sarah spends her days having conversations with imaginary cowboys and American Indians, all of which is surprisingly well-tolerated by her wonderful husband and son. Readers can find out more about Sarah's love of cowboys and Indians at www.sarahmanderson.com.

To my grandmothers, Frances, Goldie and Maggie.
I couldn't have asked for three stronger women
in my life, and for the gifts that each gave me,
I'm eternally grateful.

One

"Mr. Carlson, Agent Yellow Bird is here with Ms. Touchette." His assistant's tone was clipped and professional, giving no clue as to what sort of woman was waiting out there.

"Thank you." James's hand hovered over the old-fashioned intercom switch. The intercom wasn't his favorite way to communicate with Agnes. Reminded him too much of how his father would bark out orders to the hired help from behind the closed doors of his home office. Luckily, his father wasn't here.

And his parents had certainly never stooped to visit him in South Dakota. The sight of this shabby office in the Judicial Building in Pierre, South Dakota, would no doubt send his mother into affected hysterics. In her view, his job here was not the shortest path between the family mansion in Washington, D.C., and the White House. The Carlson family dynasty was mentioned in the same breath as the Kennedys or the Bushes. For as long as he could remember, he had been groomed for a run at the presidency. His parents expected him to do whatever it took to win. It drove them nuts that James insisted on walking the straight-and-narrow path to power instead of letting them open all the doors for him.

He picked up the photo of Ms. Touchette from his desk. The decade-old mug shot showed a bruised, beaten woman trying to look mean and mostly looking like a dog someone had kicked too many times. Her scarred skin and browned teeth were consistent with those of a meth abuser. She had a hell of a rap sheet—arrests for transporting and delivering drugs, prostitution, breaking and entering. The later arrests, which had occurred almost ten years ago, had taken place at the same time James had been finishing at the top of his class at Georgetown with seven-figure offers from all the top firms.

His father had expected him to take the highest offer, but James didn't need the money. His grandfather had left him more than enough, so James had taken an entry-level position with the Department of Justice and earned every single promotion. He was one of the best lawyers in the country not because his mother was rich or his father was powerful, but because he worked hard and followed the rules.

Not everyone followed the rules. The paper trail on Touchette went cold nine years ago. Either she'd dropped off the face of the earth or gotten better at evading the cops. Both would explain why it had taken Yellow Bird months to track her down. James hoped she'd gotten clean, but he had to remind himself that it didn't really matter what had happened to her. What mattered was that James needed her. She was an insurance policy in his quest to clean up the courtroom.

If Yellow Bird hadn't been out there, James would have let Ms. Touchette sit. Nervous people were easier to manipulate than calm people. But FBI agent Thomas Yellow Bird was no criminal. Half the time, James got the feeling Yellow Bird would drop him with one shot, given the opportunity.

The other half, James was sure the man would take a bullet for him. James preferred to stay on the latter side as much as possible. He stood to put on his suit jacket and straighten his tie. "Send Ms. Touchette in, please."

Yellow Bird entered, motioning for the woman to follow him. James remained standing—even criminals deserved common courtesy—but when she walked into his office, he did a double take.

She was not what he was expecting.

The woman standing before him had long black hair that hung to her shoulders in loose waves, with bangs that swept down low over her left eye. Her skin was a clear, tawny brown and appeared to be scar free. She wore a brown, ankle-length, tiered skirt and a pink tank top, and she clutched a brown leather bag to her side. She was clean, her eyes bright and wary. She'd look good on a witness stand.

She'd look better in bed.

Where had that come from? He hadn't had such an instinctive response to a woman in a while. But it didn't matter. James shook that inappropriate thought out of his head. She was off-limits. Because she was a potential witness, James couldn't act on any attraction to her. It was inappropriate, unethical and could get him debarred—not to mention it was the kind of thing his father would do. And even if that wasn't the case, it didn't matter how beautiful or put together she was—former hookers didn't become first ladies.

At least, he thought she was the former hooker he'd asked Yellow Bird to bring in. He looked down at the mug shot, then back at the woman. He couldn't see the slightest similarity. Yellow Bird had never been wrong before—but there was a first for everything. "I'm Special Prosecutor James Carlson. Thank you for coming, Ms. Touchette."

"I'm not Touchette." Her voice was strong—no hint of

nerves. Her eyes focused on a point behind James's shoulder. "My name is Eagle Heart."

Confused, James looked to Yellow Bird, who slouched against a filing cabinet as far off to the side as one could get in this small office. "Show him," Yellow Bird said in a low voice.

The woman didn't move.

"Maggie." The tone of Yellow Bird's voice changed, making his accent more pronounced. It was enough to be menacing. "Show him."

The woman took a deep breath as her gaze cut down to the mug shot on James's desk. "My name is Maggie Eagle Heart now," she said as she lifted the heavy bangs away from the side of her head.

She revealed a twisted knot of faded scar tissue that encroached on her hairline and sliced the edge off her eyebrow. James looked down at the mug shot and saw the matching wound. It had healed well, but the scar was still visible.

"And…" Yellow Bird said.

Ms. Eagle Heart turned, dropping one shoulder of her tank top. James's gut clenched as she revealed a wide swath of bare skin. He couldn't help it—his eyes dropped down to where the strap of her bra met the band. The rest of the shirt hugged her curves. What did her legs look like under that skirt? He wanted to see. Even though he shouldn't, he wanted to touch. But he couldn't—not now, not as long as he was a prosecutor and she was a witness.

She draped her hair over her front, revealing a tattoo that covered her right shoulder blade. In and amongst the flames, James could make out the letters that spelled "LLD." Margaret Touchette and Maggie Eagle Heart were the same woman— but different. *Very* different.

She stood, her back to him and her head held high. Under no circumstances should James find any of her actions erotic, but the way she'd dropped the strap of her top—and the bra strap underneath it… He cleared his throat and sat down to hide his lower region as he flipped through the file until he found the matching photo of the tattoo.

Damn it, this wasn't like him. He lived for his job. He never let himself get distracted by a witness. But he was distracted. What was it about her that did that to him? If he was having this much trouble just interviewing her, how hard would it be to actually work with her?

"Thank you, that will do." As much as he didn't want her to put that strap back up, he needed her to. Right now.

She turned back around, her eyes focused over his shoulder again. He motioned for her to sit as he said, "Thank you, Agent Yellow Bird. I can take it from here."

"I want Yellow Bird to stay." Again, no wobble to her voice. James was impressed.

"I can assure you, Ms. Eagle Heart, this is a strictly professional interview. The nature of what we discuss is confidential."

Her right eyebrow notched up, but otherwise, her expression stayed blank. "Easy to say. Hard to prove. Can he stay or not?"

The challenge was subtle—but it was still a challenge. This was not what James had been expecting. People who came to see him usually had something to hide. They either tried to cut a deal, be invisible or bluster their way out of the situation. In any case, they acted rashly. This woman? She was something else entirely. All Yellow Bird had said when James had asked him to find Margaret Touchette was that he'd need a little time. He hadn't said anything about *knowing* her.

James looked to Yellow Bird, who tilted his head in agreement. "Fine. Let's begin, shall we?" He motioned to the single chair in front of his desk as he turned on the digital recorder. "For the record, state your full name, *all* aliases and occupation."

She hesitated, then sat, pulling her bag onto her lap like a shield. She wrapped the strap around her fingers, then unwrapped and rewrapped them. It was the only outward sign of her anxiety. "My name is Maggie Eagle Heart. I used to be Margaret Marie Touchette, but I'm not anymore. I make dance costumes and jewelry and sell them online."

James wrote it all down. "When did you get married?"

"I'm not married."

He looked up, keeping the surprise off his face. She was available. That shouldn't matter, but the news pleased him anyway. Ms. Eagle Heart's gaze had shifted from behind him to the file on the desk. Still not looking at him, though.

"I see." He swallowed, not because he was suddenly nervous. James Carlson, special prosecutor, personally appointed by the attorney general, did not get nervous. He could trace his mother's side of the family back to the *Mayflower,* for God's sake. His grandfather had been the eighth billionaire in America, and he didn't get there by being undone by beautiful strangers. Nerves were not allowed. Not during interviews, not in the courtroom. "How do you know Agent Yellow Bird?"

She didn't say anything for a long moment. "Once upon a time, a boy named Tommy tried to save a girl named Maggie. But he couldn't. No one could."

"Are you seeing anyone now?"

Yellow Bird's head popped up, and Ms. Eagle Heart's eyes focused on his face for the first time. James's wildly inappropriate question hung in the silence. He swallowed again. He shouldn't have asked it—but he wanted to know.

Her eyes were a warm, intelligent brown, and more than a little wary. Her chin tilted to one side as she weighed his inquiry. Suddenly, he felt as if she had all the power in the room. The back of his neck began to sweat. "I'm not seeing anyone. What's this about?"

Not married. Not even taken. Why did that matter? "When did you adopt your current alias?" Yes. He needed to get this train back on track. He was the one asking the questions around here. He was in charge.

Her eyes took on a distance, and she stopped looking at him. "Nine years ago."

Right after her last arrest. He looked her over again—not because she was a lovely woman. That had nothing to do with it. He was merely trying to gauge her willingness to cooperate. "How long was that after your last trial date?"

Her eyes fluttered shut, but her head didn't drop. "Do I need a lawyer?"

He glanced down at the defeated woman in the mug shot again. The woman before him? Anything but defeated.

"No, although I can recommend one of the best attorneys in the state, if you'd like." He dug around in the top drawer until he found one of Rosebud Armstrong's cards and scooted it across the desk. "Agent Yellow Bird can personally vouch for her."

Of course, James knew Rosebud personally, too. But few people knew that the son former secretary of defense Alex Carlson and his wife, Julia, had been prepping for public office since he was born had had an affair with a Lakota Indian woman throughout law school. That was the sort of information that, if the media bloodhounds got a hold of it, could be twisted around until it destroyed a nascent political career before it got off the ground. James had worked too hard for too long to let something as base as physical desire ruin everything. He just needed to keep reminding himself of that fact every time he looked at Ms. Eagle Heart.

Without raising her eyes, Ms. Eagle Heart closed one hand around the card. James thought she'd put it in her bag, but she held on to it, running the pad of her thumb over the edge. Interesting, James thought. She couldn't keep her hands still.

Her fingertips were long, with clean, short nails that showed no sign of polish. Her hands had a few calluses. Those were not the hands of a pampered, coddled woman—a woman like Pauline Walker, the woman his mother had hand-picked to be James's own blank slate of a wife. No, Ms. Eagle Heart had the hands of a woman who knew how to use them.

James shifted in his chair. Back on track. Now.

"Ms. Eagle Heart, the reason I've called you in for this interview today is because I think you have personal knowledge of a crime that was committed, and I would like to confirm your version of events."

The color drained from her face. "I don't know anything about any criminal activity. I'm innocent. I was never convicted."

"Despite being arrested seventeen times, yes. I noted that. I also noted that you had the same judge for all of your court appearances. One Royce T. Maynard."

James's pulse began to race as his train not only got back on track, but picked up a head of steam. Maynard was, hands down, the most crooked judge ever to sit on the bench outside of New York City. Putting criminals like Maynard away would be the biggest feather in James's cap. And after this case was resolved, James would resign his position with the Department of Justice and launch upon his political career with ironclad credentials as the man who would clean up government. He'd start by running for attorney general, then governor, and then—if things went according to plan—higher positions. Ones that came with nice roomy oval offices.

Early on, James hadn't understood why his parents insisted he had to be president. He could do a lot of good in the world as a lawyer, as contradictory as that sounded. Lawyers fought for truth, justice and the American way—at least, that's how it had seemed back when he'd been a kid, eavesdropping on his parents' cocktail parties. Lawyers bragged about the big victories they won, whereas elected officials were always complaining about the red tape they had to battle and the re-election campaigns they had to run. Lawyers were the winners. Elected officials were tomorrow's punching bags.

As an adult, James had realized that lawyers could lose just as easily as they won, and that politicians did have the power to change the world—if they didn't let themselves get corrupted by special interests and lobbyists. James could guide this country the way he prosecuted his cases—efficiently, cleanly and with justice for the American people first and foremost in his mind. But to do that, he needed to have an unimpeachable background. No scandals, no skeletons, no questionable relationships with questionable women.

Women like Maggie Eagle Heart.

First things first. James had to prove Maynard's guilt in a court of law. To do that, he needed the testimony of unreliable witnesses like Maggie Eagle Heart. Except that the woman sitting on the other side of his desk wasn't exactly unreliable. In fact, with her alert eyes, set shoulders and unflinching confidence, she looked exactly like the kind of woman James would like to get to know better.

Ms. Eagle Heart swallowed. "Who?" She said it in a way that was supposed to make it sound as if she'd never heard Maynard's name before, but, for the first time, her voice wobbled.

"I'm curious as to why a woman who was mixed up with the wrong crowd would walk away scot-free seventeen times. Once or twice, sure. But seventeen?"

"I don't know what you're talking about." The wobble was stronger this time.

He had her dead to rights. "I think you do, Ms. Eagle Heart. I think you know why you're here today, and I think you know what I want." He shouldn't have said that last bit, because her gaze zeroed in on him through thick lashes, the challenge writ large on her face. James knew in that instant she understood what he wanted—both in and out of the courtroom.

She didn't offer up another weak protest, though. She kept right on looking at him with that combination of knowledge and distance. She was challenging him again. She wasn't going to make this easy.

Yellow Bird shifted against the far wall, breaking the tension of the moment.

"The Department of Justice believes that Royce T. Maynard regularly abused the power of his office. He solicited and received bribes, took payments to sway judgments in courtrooms other than his own and…" James didn't want to say this out loud, but as Ms. Eagle Heart wasn't exactly jumping in, he forged ahead. "And pressured defendants to exchange services in return for judgments in their favor."

She got a little paler. "Are you accusing me of a crime?"

"Not directly. We believe that Maynard demanded certain services in return for letting you off the hook." He tossed the deposition of one of Maynard's former bailiffs across the desk—the one that outlined how Maynard regularly recessed court so he could meet with female defendants in his chambers *without* their counsel.

She didn't move, not even her hands. James wasn't sure if she was breathing. He felt like the world's biggest jerk. He couldn't say what this woman had been doing for most of the last decade, but it seemed clear that she'd made a different sort of life for herself than the one the woman in the mug shot had chosen. However, his moment of regret was short-lived. He hadn't gotten to be the youngest special prosecutor in the history of the DOJ by worrying about witnesses' feelings.

"This is from a former public defender," he added, handing over another deposition that detailed how the man who gave lawyers a bad name encouraged his clients accused of prostitution—including one Margaret Touchette—to go into chambers alone, where he believed they performed sex acts for Maynard in return for a not-guilty judgment. "I believe you'll recognize the name."

Her hand shaking, Ms. Eagle Heart picked up the deposition and read the name. Slowly, she set the file back down on the desk and took a deep breath. Her hair hung over the side of her face with the scar. With that identifying mark hidden, James couldn't see anything about her that said *drug addict* or *prostitute*. Maggie Eagle Heart was a composed, beautiful woman who didn't spook easily. He admired her resolve, but he'd be lying if he didn't admit there was something else that drew him to her. Too bad he couldn't spend a little time exploring what that something else was, but there was no way in hell he would jeopardize his entire career just because he was taken with her.

"Why am I here?" The wobble was gone from her voice. Instead, she was just flat-out pissed. Her eyes flashed with defiance. "You have the official testimony of two people. You don't need me or the testimony you think I have."

"That's where you're wrong. What I have is the second-hand testimony of two people who were never present when the alleged crimes occurred. Because that's what they were, Ms. Eagle Heart. Crimes. It is illegal for officers of the court to demand favors from defendants, especially sexual favors. I'm working to eliminate criminals from our justice system so that people like Margaret Touchette can get a fair trial and the real help they need. And to do that, I need the testimony of a firsthand witness. I need you to describe how Maynard approached you and what he demanded from you in return for those seventeen not-guilty verdicts."

"No."

James smiled at her, making sure all his teeth were showing. His feral smile, Agnes called it. It straddled the line between polite and menacing and was quite effective in the courtroom. "Ms. Eagle Heart, at this point, you're not being charged with a crime. But that could change."

She met his gaze with one of steely determination. "So, if I understand you correctly, you've approached me and are demanding a favor in return for a not-guilty verdict. How delightfully hypocritical of you. I've learned to expect nothing less from the law."

She stood. James knew he should cut off whatever else she was going to say and keep control of the conversation, but he wanted to hear what she was going to throw at him. A string of curse words? Would she slap him?

"The statute of limitations on anything Margaret Touchette did or did not do has expired. You can't charge me. You can't hold me. The next time you want to talk me, don't send your dog after me." She turned to Yellow Bird. "I want to go home now." And with that, she opened the door and made a quiet, dignified exit.

She'd called his bluff. She'd known it was a bluff from the beginning.

James let out a low whistle of appreciation, causing Yellow Bird to glance at him before he walked out. Seconds later, the outer door of the office shut.

Well, hell. That hadn't gone according to plan, but he was impressed with her. Most women in her position would have crumbled. Hell, he'd seen professional lawyers buckle when cornered, but not her. She had an entire closet full of skeletons, but she didn't let anyone judge her because of it, and she didn't let it compromise her position. James had to admire her. She had come up firing and left him wanting more.

He weighed his options. He couldn't let her off the hook— he needed her testimony in his back pocket, just in case. If he sent Yellow Bird back after her, she'd probably clam up and refuse to talk, much less to testify. That only left one option.

Agnes stepped into his office, appointment book in hand. "Shall I put the young lady back on the interview schedule?"

His feral smile didn't work on Agnes any better than it had on Maggie Eagle Heart, but he tried it out anyway. "Get me her address." As long as he had a legitimate reason to see her, he wasn't acting unethically. Convincing her to testify wasn't throwing his hard work away, it was building his case. As long as he remembered that, he'd be fine. He needed her as a witness, and that meant he'd have to see her again.

It was just that simple.

Two

The black sedan peeled out of the parking lot and took a left so sharply that Maggie thought they might have gone up on two wheels. Agent Yellow Bird kept driving like a bat out of hell, weaving around traffic and running stale yellow lights at speeds more fitting to a police chase than a ride home, all of which made one thing clear.

Tommy was mad at her.

A tendril of forgotten fear curled around her stomach. She hated the feeling of having done something wrong. She'd learned early that bad things happened when people got mad. When she'd been small, she had hidden under her bed, until that became the first place her uncle looked. When she got older, she crashed on whatever empty couch she could, trying to avoid home altogether. And when that failed, well, drugs had taken her away like nothing else had. Except that they'd taken away everything else, too.

For a long time, it had been a trade-off she'd been willing to make. Not anymore. Not for the last nine years.

Was she nervous? Oh, yes. Tommy had grown into a formidable man since she'd seen him last, and that wasn't counting the gun he wore under his jacket. Was she going to hide and whimper and beg for mercy?

Hell, no.

But she wasn't about to confront him while he took corners as if they were an insult to his manhood. She'd wait until they were on the highway, headed home through the long, flat parts of South Dakota.

Her thoughts turned to the conversation with James Carlson, special prosecutor. She'd known when Tommy showed up on her doorstep that someone had realized who she was. She'd been expecting another fat, sweaty, *greedy* man like the Dishonorable Royce T. Maynard to preside over the interview. Not the handsome man with the kind eyes and sharp smile.

Special Prosecutor Carlson had sat there with her mug shots in front of him and looked at her with something that wasn't disapproval and wasn't quite lust—not entirely, anyway. If she hadn't known any better, she might have guessed that he'd looked at her with respect.

But she did know better. She didn't trust lawyers.

Still, that Carlson had seemed different from the other men she'd endured in the past. For one, he'd walked a fine line between good-looking and gorgeous. Having paid several thousand dollars to get her own teeth fixed, she appreciated a good set of pearly whites. He had the kind of smile that made it clear that he—or his parents—had spent a lot of money on getting them perfect.

For another thing, his suit fit as if it had been made for him. Maybe it had been, but she'd never had a lawyer who could afford a custom suit. The slime bag who'd given Carlson her name had always worn hideous brown suits that looked as though he'd stolen them off the clothesline of some taller, wider man. But not Carlson. His charcoal-gray suit sat on his shoulders like a second skin. She could tell that, underneath all that expensive wool, he was a well-built man. Broad shoulders, strong arms—from the waist up, he was gorgeous. She couldn't help wondering what he looked like from the waist down.

Maggie slammed the door on that kind of thinking. There was nothing wrong with a man being attractive. Nothing wrong with noticing an attractive man. But that's as far as it could go. She couldn't afford to forget what he was—a lawyer. Lawyers—and judges—used people. She knew that better than anyone, and she was done being used. As long as she remembered who he was—and who she wasn't—she'd be fine. If she ever saw him again.

Maybe she would. So she hadn't been with a man in years. She'd still recognized something in his face after she'd pulled the strap of her tank top down, and she'd recognized the same something when he'd asked her if she was seeing anyone. Not quite lust, but desire. Interest, mixed with pleasant surprise— curiosity, maybe—when she'd thrown down her challenge. When she'd called Tommy a dog.

Hence the pissed silence at the speed of sound.

She wasn't about to let Tommy out of her sight without getting him to tell her what he knew. "You're mad at me."

"I'm not his dog."

"I see." She'd known that comment would hit home. But she'd been angry. Tommy had been quiet the entire trip to Pierre, telling her nothing about where they were going or who wanted to see her. He'd earned a few hits. "What are you, then?"

"We're partners. A team." His fingers kept drumming. "I arrest people, he puts them away. That's how it works."

"Since you're on his team, tell me—will I be seeing Special

Prosecutor James Carlson again?" Even saying his title out loud gave her a weird feeling in the pit of her stomach.

"Yep."

She couldn't imagine anything good coming from that, but the news excited her anyway. She'd get to see that smile again. "Why does he need me? Surely Maynard left bigger and better loose ends." That was the question that had nagged at her since Carlson had made his preposterous claim that his whole case rested on her.

"He doesn't need you. He's the kind of man who has a plan for every contingency. You're what he calls an insurance policy. He likes to have a few, just in case."

That struck her wrong. She was a person—a woman, damn it. For too long, she'd been a victim, a statistic—never just Maggie. She wouldn't stand for having her hard-fought success downgraded to "backup plan."

"I'd give him a week, eight days tops, before he shows up. What you do with him then is up to you."

Maggie's head popped up and she stared at Tommy. "What?" Because that had almost sounded like…hell, she didn't know. A joke? Permission to shoot? Permission to…do something else? No telling. Tommy didn't answer, so Maggie tried again. "Tell me about him." Not because she wanted to know, but because she needed to be prepared if he was going to trek out to the house. Yes, that was a good reason—one that had nothing to do with anything above—or below—his waist. She couldn't be interested in him because there was no way in hell she could trust him.

"Nice guy, unless you're on the wrong side of the law. Blue-blooded, East Coast, rich. His mother has the fortune, but his father has the power—maybe you've heard of him? Alexander Carlson? Used to be the secretary of defense?"

Maggie swallowed. She was *way* out of her league here. Secretary of defense? Alex Carlson? Even Maggie knew who that was. That wasn't just blue blood or rich. That was pure power. His father had launched *wars,* for crying out loud. Even if James had not been a lawyer she couldn't trust, she wouldn't dream of fantasizing about him now. He wasn't just a lawyer. He was a *somebody*—and she wasn't. "Yeah, I've heard of him."

"Carlson is just biding his time," Tommy went on. "We've been building this case for about four years, and he won't let anything sink it. He needs this victory. Going to run for office after he wins. Sooner or later—sooner, if I know him— he'll make a run at the White House."

The air in Maggie's lungs stopped moving. So she'd had a conversation with a possible future president of the United States today. And she'd told him off. That sickening feeling of having done something wrong got a lot stronger. "He's going to win?" The case, the elections—one and the same, as far as she was concerned.

Tommy snorted. "He's got a perfect track record. He'll win it one way or another."

That sounded ominous. How ridiculous was she to think that a man like him was looking at her with desire? A man like him had perfect women at his beck and call. Maggie was so far from perfect that she wasn't even in the same zip code. "Do you trust him?"

Tommy gave her a sideways glance. "With my life." It could have sounded flip, but he was dead serious. "You got that card he gave you?"

She dug around in her bag until she found it. "Yes." Rosebud Armstrong, Attorney at Law. There was a phone number, but that was it. No address, no law-firm name. Fate had a sense of humor. She'd escaped from the Rosebud reservation. Now her life might rest in the hands of a woman with the same name.

"You can trust her. She's Red Creek Lakota—my tribe.

And she went to law school with Carlson. She knows how he thinks. If you want a lawyer, you tell her I sent you."

Of course, Tommy also knew how Carlson thought, being as they were on the same team and all—and what had that gotten her? Nothing. "I don't want to call her. I don't want any of this. I have a normal life now, and you and your 'team' are threatening to ruin it—and for what? Because that stuck-up spoiled brat of a lawyer wants an insurance policy? No. I'm nobody's bargaining chip. I refuse."

Although she was in danger of pouting, she crossed her arms and stared straight ahead. Which made the laughter that suddenly burst out of Tommy that much more startling.

His reaction only made her madder. "You can go to hell, Thomas Yellow Bird, because you *are* a dog. You didn't have to find me. What happens when word gets out, huh? And don't give me any bull about confidentiality. What happens when Leonard Low Dog or my uncle find out I'm not dead?"

"Nothing."

"You know that for sure—how? You going to put a bullet in their brains for me?"

"Low Dog is doing twenty to life in Leavenworth, and your uncle lost both his legs and his eyesight to diabetes a couple of years ago."

"Leonard's in prison?" And her uncle was legless. She shouldn't feel so happy at this news, but she couldn't deny the relief that made her want to jump up and shout. They couldn't get to her. She was safe.

Tommy gave her a long look. "I put him there, about seven years ago. You were gone by then. I asked around, but everyone said you'd died."

"You didn't believe that?"

"Nope."

Which explained why James Carlson would have even

bothered to look for her. Yellow Bird had promised he could find her. "How *did* you find me?"

"I got lucky." He didn't elaborate, damn him.

"That's it? You're not even going to tell me how you tracked me down?"

"Nope."

"Fine." She smoothed out her skirt again before she caught herself, so she folded her arms to keep her hands quiet. "Be that way."

A flood of conflicting emotions threatened to swamp her. James Carlson was threatening her because she was nothing more than an uncooperative insurance policy. But there'd been more to his interest than that of a prosecutor. Had he really been curious about who she was seeing, or had he just been using flattery to manipulate her into doing what he wanted?

They pulled up in front of the house Nan had built into a low hill. She kept the front half whitewashed, but the back end of the place was completely sunk into the earth. Sure, it was dusty in the summer, but it stayed cool in the summer and warmish in the winter. Maggie had always taken comfort in the fact that no one could sneak in a back way. There was no back way, just hill. They were close enough to Aberdeen that they had nice things like television reception and internet connectivity, but far enough away that they couldn't see any other lights after dark. That isolation had been exactly what Maggie had needed.

Tommy put the car in Park, but he didn't turn it off. She still had so many questions. "*Why* did you find me?"

His fingers drummed on the steering wheel again. "I wanted to know what happened to you."

She'd be lying if she didn't admit she'd wondered what had happened to him, too. "Like I told *him* once upon a time, a boy named Tommy tried to save a girl named Maggie. But he couldn't. No one could."

Tommy looked at her, a sad smile pulling on his mouth. "No one could. She had to save herself." He reached over and touched her cheek. "Carlson's a good guy, but you do what you've got to do."

"Okay." It was going to be okay. She'd told herself that for years, hoping that hope alone would make it so, but suddenly, she knew with certainty that it would be okay. She could do anything. Even handle a special prosecutor.

She got out of the car. Agent Yellow Bird waited until she was at the front door before he took off at chase speeds again.

Maggie stood there for a moment, feeling a lightness that matched the orange glow of the sunset. She looked out over the land that was her home now, over the rows of vegetables she'd have to weed tomorrow and the windmill that powered the water pump. Suddenly, after today's events, she didn't feel as though she had to hide out here anymore. Just the same, though, she wanted to stay. This was her life.

Nan was where she always was, sitting in her recliner and watching *Deadliest Catch*. "Well?" she said without lifting her eyes from the pillow she was embroidering.

"Low Dog is in prison and my uncle is blind and in a wheelchair."

Nan's needle paused in midair. "So, good news, then?"

"That part, at least. A special prosecutor wants me to testify against that judge." She left out the part about the prosecutor being handsome and rich and powerful.

Nan made a tsking noise and kept sewing. If Maggie hadn't seen the pictures of Nan as a young woman with freckles and fiery-red hair, she wouldn't believe the woman before her wasn't an Indian. She had everything—the way she wore her hair, the clothes she chose, even the way she talked—down pat. The sun had tanned her face and hands a leathery brown, and she was an expert on Sioux traditions.

"I see. What did he offer you?"

Maggie pulled up short. "Nothing."

The needle paused again. "Nothing?"

"Well, he offered not to charge me."

Nan tsked again. "Must not be a very special prosecutor if he didn't give you anything you wanted."

Maggie sat down in her chair with a thump. "I think he's a good lawyer. I just think he was expecting someone else." He was expecting a woman who had exchanged sex acts for not-guilty verdicts. His offer had been for that woman. Maggie wasn't that woman anymore. "Besides, he doesn't have anything I want."

That was dangerously close to a lie. He did have something she wanted—that smile, those eyes, and all those muscles underneath that suit. But she didn't *want* to want them. If she wanted them—him—and if he figured that out, he could use it against her. He could use her. As much as she wanted to see James Carlson again, she had to protect herself from him. There was no way in hell she'd put herself back into a position where someone else was calling her shots. Those days were over.

"You okay, sweetie?" Nan finally looked up, the concern bright in her eyes.

Maggie thought back to the stunned look on his face when she'd stood up to him—when she'd stood up for herself. She hadn't been what he'd been expecting, but then, she hadn't expected anyone to look at her with such honesty. Would James Carlson come looking for her?

She hoped so. She shouldn't, but she did anyway.

"Yeah," she said. "I think I am."

Three

The sun beat down on Maggie's head. The wide brim of her floppy straw hat kept the back of her neck from burning, but on days like this, she had half a mind to take her pruning knife and whack her braids off. It was just that damn hot.

Maggie dropped a shovel full of composted manure onto the freshly tilled garden soil. She shouldn't whine about the sun—it had dried the stink right out of the manure. She stood up and tried to stretch the kinks out of her back as she looked at the sky. If only she and Mother Nature could compromise on the occasional cloud…

She was halfway through the rest of her wheelbarrow when she heard it—the crunching of tires on gravel from a long way off. The hair on the back of her neck stood straight up. *Wonderful,* she thought. Tommy had been wrong. It had only been four days since she'd left James Carlson's office in a huff—not eight. And here she was, covered in dirt and manure. Damn. She snatched her hat off her head and arranged her bangs over the side of her face. Individual hairs stuck to her skin, but her scar was hidden.

At least, she hoped it was James Carlson, despite the ratty overalls she was wearing. She didn't want to think about who else it could be on a Saturday afternoon. Despite Tommy's reassurances, Maggie was reasonably sure there were a few other people in this world who'd want to see her for all the wrong reasons.

She glanced back at the house, wondering if Nan could hear the approaching car over the TV. If so, she'd have the shotgun at the ready. A girl couldn't be too careful, after all.

A shiny black SUV—the kind that looked as if it had never been on gravel before—hesitantly worked its way down to the house. She leaned on the handle of her shovel and watched it come.

Maggie smiled. So that was the kind of "off-road" vehicle that rich, East Coast blue bloods bought when they were roughing it. She'd stick to her Jeep, thank you.

"You're a long way from home," she called out when Mr. Special Prosecutor himself emerged from the driver's seat.

The first thing she saw was the blinding white of his smile. *Wow,* she thought again. That smile wasn't quite as sharp as it had been in the office. If anything, he almost looked glad to see her. Then she noticed that, instead of the suit, he had on a pair of tan cargo pants and a sky-blue polo shirt. Even though the clothes were pretty casual, they fit him well.

Broad chest, she thought with a sharp intake of breath. Without the jacket, she could see exactly how broad—and defined—his chest was, and how it narrowed into the V of his waist.

Whoa. Not just attractive. Downright gorgeous.

Heat—different from the swelter that had sweat dripping down the back of her neck—ripped through her, and she suddenly found herself doing some crude math. Exactly how long had it been since her last time with a man? No—wrong question. How long had it been since she'd last enjoyed a man?

His eyes were shaded behind wraparound sunglasses, but he leaned forward and slid them down his nose to look at her.

Way too long, she thought. Maybe never.

"I believe I was invited," he called as he pulled something out of the backseat.

Sheesh. Only a lawyer would construe what she'd said as an invitation. "Did Yellow Bird tell you how to find me?"

He was carrying something. As he got closer, she saw that it was a bright orange garden trug, loaded with stuff. "Not too many people get away with calling him names." He grinned at her, as if he was letting her in on some secret. "Here. I brought you something." He set the trug in between the rows and took a step back.

She looked at him for a long second. Was this a gift, or a bribe?

"It's a gift. No strings attached."

Tommy hadn't said anything about mind reading. Keeping an eye on her visitor, Maggie crouched down. Deerskin gardening gloves, a trowel with an ergonomic handle, copper garden tags, a matching copper watering can and a bunch of heirloom seeds were all nestled inside. All top-quality stuff that she would never waste money on. She lifted out the watering can. Was this a Hawes? She'd seen this one in catalogs—for a hundred and forty dollars.

The whole basket must have set him back close to five hundred. James Carlson was, in fact, a good lawyer. At the very least, a rich one.

"I can't accept this." Even as she said it, she picked up the gloves. The leather was softer than anything else she owned. These weren't the everyday gloves they sold at the hardware store. "I won't testify."

"I didn't say anything about testifying. I said it was a gift.

I wouldn't come to pay my respects empty-handed. I know better."

She looked up at him. His feet were spread a shoulder's width apart, his arms were crossed, and a cryptic smile graced his face. He looked like a man who reigned over everything he saw, and right now, he was looking at her.

Goose bumps shot up her arms. She swallowed as she stood. She didn't want anyone—least of all him—to think she was kneeling before him. Not too many people knew about the Lakota tradition of giving gifts. "Yellow Bird tell you that, too?"

"It's something I picked up along the way." He turned around, taking in her garden. "This is lovely." Then he caught sight of the wheelbarrow. "Is that what I think it is?"

She glared at him. "My garden is organic. Did you come all the way out here to compliment my vegetables?"

He managed not to be offended at her short temper. Instead, he almost looked as if he enjoyed her attitude. "No. I came to see you."

There it was again—the feeling that wasn't quite lust, but wasn't entirely innocent, either. What she wouldn't give to *not* be in overalls, or standing next to a manure-filled wheelbarrow. "Yellow Bird said you'd show up." Which was probably a stupid thing to say, but she had to say something.

Oh. My. That particular smile lit up his whole face. "The fact that Yellow Bird said anything is impressive. Either your interrogation tactics are unparalleled, or he's fond of you."

Anger hit her like a bolt out of the blue. "I didn't sleep with him, if that's what you mean." The words flew out of her mouth faster than she could figure out what she was saying. She grabbed the shovel and swung it onto her shoulder as if it was a baseball bat. She could take the head off a snake in seconds. At the very least, she'd break his nose. "I'm not like that anymore, so if that's why you're here, you can take your stuff and go back the way you came."

Looking a little stunned, he held up his hands and took two steps back. "I'm not implying anything. I can't believe Yellow Bird would be fond of anyone. Half the time, I think he wants to shoot me."

She eyed him. Lawyers were prone to lying. Was he telling the truth or saving his backside? "'Fond'? Who talks like that?"

A hint of red graced his cheeks, and Maggie immediately regretted her snippiness. At this exact moment in time, the man standing before her didn't look—or act—like any lawyer she'd ever known.

Nice, she scolded herself as her own blush began to creep down her chest. *Way to embarrass yourself.* Was there any way to salvage this situation without acting like a total jerk?

She took the shovel off her shoulder and set it on the ground. In response, he lowered his hands. An uneasy silence settled over them. God, she was so out of practice. She didn't talk to anyone but Nan, and Jemma over at the post office. Was she supposed to apologize now or what?

"Let's start over," he said, offering his hand. "Hi. I'm James."

Start over? Just like that? If only life were that simple. Maybe it was. He stood there with a soft grin on his face as he leaned forward in anticipation. "Maggie," she replied. Although she wasn't sure it was a good idea, she placed her hand in his and gave it a short shake.

Not a good idea. Warmth that had nothing to do with embarrassment began a slow build from where their skin touched. She meant to let go, but she was paralyzed by the oddity of the sensation. Tingles followed the warmth as it moved up her arm. The combination of the two was enough to squeeze the air out of her chest.

Nope. Not allowed. She forcibly regained control of her limbs and wrenched her hand out of his. So what if James was hot? So what if he had a good smile? So what if he made her feel things she'd forgotten she was capable of feeling? He was off-limits. He was probably trying to manipulate her. He was some East Coast rich guy, so he'd never be able to understand what her life had been before, or what it was now. He was going to be the president one day, so she could never in a million, billion years entertain the notion of kissing James Carlson. Not even once.

"It's nice to meet you, Maggie." He didn't seem offended by her reaction. She couldn't decide if he was that smooth, or merely that clueless. "Tell me about yourself."

She needed to get her head together. It might be difficult, if not impossible, to do it while he was standing here, looking untouched by the blazing sun or the proximity to manure, but she needed to try. And to do that, she needed a drink. "There's lemonade in the house, if you're interested." Tea would have been more traditional, but hey—it was eighty-seven degrees out. And then she could at least wash her hands and face while Nan sized him up.

"That would be lovely." He stepped to the side to let her pass and then followed her into the house.

When she opened the door, Nan was in her chair, as usual, but Maggie noted the way she was breathing a little hard. She made a casual turn in order to check that the door had shut behind James and spotted the shotgun nestled in between the umbrellas. Good ol' Nan. She always, *always* had Maggie's back. "Nan, I'd like you to meet James Carlson. James, this is Nanette Brown." She left it at that.

Nan managed to stand without knocking over her worktable. "Welcome, welcome." She gave Maggie a look that said *you look like hell*. "Can I get you some lemonade?"

Maggie took her cue and ran with it. "Excuse me." She

sprinted back to the bathroom, where she furiously scrubbed every available surface with a scratchy washcloth. Without bothering to dry herself off—water evaporated—she bolted to her room and dug out a clean pair of jeans and the nicest top she owned, the blue silk one with the bugle beads around the neck. She'd have to act as if the wrinkles were meant to be there.

When she got to the kitchen, James was leaning up against the counter while Nan rummaged in the fridge. "I know I've got some cake in here—oh! There it is," the older woman mumbled at the lettuce crisper as she rooted around for the leftover carrot cake.

James glanced—and then stared—at her. "Hi," he said again, sounding more like a regular guy than a lawyer.

Maggie swallowed. He was probably used to high-class women who had perfect manicures and could subsist on celery for months at a time, women whose spring wardrobes cost more than her car. It wasn't possible that he was attracted to her. It just wasn't. She had dirt—or worse—wedged under her fingernails, and she saw too late that the jeans she'd grabbed had a smear of paint down the thigh. "Hi."

Over the next five minutes, Nan bustled around the kitchen, slicing cake and pouring lemonade as she tossed out harmless small talk such as, "It's so hot out! And they say we aren't going to get any rain until the weekend."

Throughout the verbal barrage, James nodded and smiled and agreed as if they were all the oldest of friends. Maggie felt horribly out of place in her own kitchen. She wasn't wearing a skirt to smooth out, so she had nothing to do but sit on her hands.

"Oh, my—look at the time!" Nan made a clucking sound as she gathered up her cake and lemonade. "*The Biker Brotherhood* is on! I'll close the doors so my show doesn't interrupt you two." Before Maggie could protest, Nan had the bifold doors shut.

They were alone. "It's her favorite show," Maggie explained, looking at her cake. Strangely, she had no appetite.

James didn't notice. "She seems sweet. Are you two related?"

"She's sort of my fairy godmother." Which sounded so much better than, "She found me when I was a Popsicle and nursed me back to health."

James grinned as he took another bite of cake. "This is delicious."

More of that unfamiliar warmth heated her cheeks. "Thanks."

"You made it?" He looked surprised—but as though it was a good surprise.

"I like to bake." Lord knew she had enough practice. There wasn't much else to do out here in the winter.

He finished his cake and sat back, taking in the cramped confines of the kitchen. "This is a nice place."

Now he was sucking up. "Compared to what?" She couldn't know for sure, but she was willing to bet rich boys didn't spend a lot of time in earth houses.

Why on God's green earth did he keep smiling at her? Had she missed some manure on her forehead or what? "Compared to a lot of places. How long have you been here?"

"Nine years. The whole time."

"It suits you."

"What's that supposed to mean?"

James let out a low chuckle as he leaned forward and looked her straight in the eyes. "Maggie, please. I'm not interrogating you, and I'm not about to try to bluff you again. I hope you can forgive me for assuming that you would be less intelligent and less beautiful than you are. My information was sorely out of date. I promise I won't underestimate you again."

The tension she'd been holding in rushed out of her in a loud whoosh. That was, hands down, the best compliment she'd ever gotten. She knew she was blushing, but she couldn't help it, not when he was close enough to touch, looking at her with that mix of respect and desire.

"Why are you here?" The words came out a little shaky, so she cleared her throat and hoped that would help.

"I need you." His words, on the other hand, were strong and sure. There wasn't a trace of doubt in them.

Rationally, she knew he was talking about the big court case and his insurance policy. He needed her *testimony*— that was all. But the way his gaze searched her face? Nothing about that said *legalese*.

"I can't do it." Stupid voice, she mentally kicked herself. Why couldn't she sound as confident as he did? It didn't matter *how* he needed her. She couldn't be swayed with compliments.

He leaned back, looking not disappointed at all. In fact, he seemed almost amused. "Did you call that lawyer?"

"No." Although, clearly, her strategy of ignoring this whole situation in the hopes that it would go away hadn't worked. "I can't afford a lawyer."

"She'll do it pro bono. And she'll tell you the same thing I am. I'm not asking you to go before the court and make a public statement. All I want is a deposition. We'll meet in my office with a court reporter. I'll ask you some questions. You'll answer them honestly. No one else will be there. No one else will know you'll be there, unless you tell them."

That didn't sound as bad as the *Law and Order*–style scenario she'd envisioned. "Pro bono—that means free, right?"

"Right." At least he had the decency not to act as if that simple question was an agreement. "It'll be a couple of hours of your life. If the case goes as I think it will, your name will never even come up in court. You'll never have to see me again." He paused. "Not if you don't want to."

She couldn't meet his unwavering gaze. Part of Maggie wanted to get the hell out of this kitchen and as far away from this unusual man as she could. Nothing good could come of anything that involved him and his mixed signals. She wasn't some pliable little girl anymore. She was a smart, intelligent woman now, the kind of woman who made wise decisions, stood on her own two feet and never, ever did anything regrettable. And no matter how sexy and understanding James was, and no matter how much she might want to find out what those muscles looked like, doing *anything* with him would be regrettable.

She peeked up at him. He was still watching her, waiting for some sort of response. Maybe she'd take it back. Would one regrettable action really be so bad?

"You don't have to make a decision right now," he finally said into the silence. "But I would like you to call Rosebud and talk to her. She can help you explore your options and walk you through the process."

Something Nan had said came back to her. "Why should I?" Gardening supplies were nice and all, but she wouldn't be bought off so cheaply. She wasn't cheap anymore.

Something in his smile sharpened, and James began to look a little bit dangerous. "That's a good question. You should because it's the right thing to do. You're a good person, Maggie—an honest, decent woman. I can see that. You run your own business and pay your bills. And because you are, you'll do this because you know you'll be making the world a little better, a little safer. So, good question. But not the correct one. The correct question is—what's in it for you? Am I right?"

It wasn't fair to make her feel guilty for looking out for

herself, but he had done just that while simultaneously complimenting the hell out of her. She nodded.

He crossed his arms, his smile growing ever sharper. "You may have been not guilty, but you still have an arrest record. I can make that whole rap sheet disappear. Margaret Touchette disappeared, after all. Her record should disappear with her."

Maggie knew she shouldn't react, but she couldn't stop the "Really?" that escaped from her lips. Starting over, just like *that*.

One of his eyebrows lifted a little. It made him look thoughtful. "Most people do not get notice when certain persons are released from prison. However, I can guarantee that if one Leonard Low Dog ever sees the free light of day again, you'd know well in advance."

Oh. *That*. That could be a useful thing, but she felt ashamed that was even a bargaining chip. So much for starting over. She kept her mouth shut, though. She wished Nan was in here. First off, Nan would see that James was a very good lawyer. He'd figured out what she wanted and needed, and was prepared to exchange it for her testimony. But more than that, she'd know what Maggie should do next.

James made a huffing noise, as if Maggie were twisting his arm when all she was doing was sitting here and getting confused. "In the event that certain persons, such as Low Dog, do manage to locate you, I would be willing to move you—new name, new place. At no cost to you."

"Pro bono," she whispered as she stared at the forgotten cake, as if it held all the answers. He was offering to protect her. No one but Nan had ever protected her. Tommy had tried, but… "For how long? Does the offer stand, I mean?" That sounded like something Nan would ask. She was proud of herself for coming up with it all by herself.

"As long as it takes."

She did some quick math. Low Dog might be in his forties. "Until he dies?"

"If that's what it takes, yes."

That was a hell of a promise. She could see James in twenty years—the president of the freaking United States personally guaranteeing the safety and well-being of a nameless Indian woman.

But Tommy trusted him—with his life, he'd said. James Carlson was a man of his word—assuming, of course, that Tommy was, as well.

A couple of hours of her time—and in exchange, she'd get her whole life back. Margaret Touchette would be dead and gone, for good this time. She wouldn't have to worry anymore. She'd finally be free of all the stupid mistakes she'd made in the past.

"I'll inform Rosebud of the terms of my offer in writing," he said. "She'll be able to explain the full implications of this offer." He leaned forward then, stretching out his hand until he touched her shoulder. He gave it a squeeze, sending that unusual warmth cascading down her back. If she could stop blushing in front of this man... "Please call her. If not for me, then for yourself. Will you promise me that?"

She shouldn't have looked up at him then, but she did. He was close enough that she could see the brown flecks in his hazel eyes and the faint scattering of freckles that were almost the same color as his skin.

He was close enough to touch.

She didn't. Instead, she stood up. His hand fell away from her, but his eyes stayed on hers. "I'll call," she promised.

What else could she do?

Four

The law office of Rosebud Armstrong was in a nice building—high ceilings, marble flooring and polished mahogany. Everything about it said money. Lots of it.

Maggie thought about bailing. She didn't belong in a place like this, and God only knew how much this meeting was going to cost. Yes, James had said pro bono, but someone had to pay. Marble didn't come cheap.

The receptionist immediately ushered her into the office. The woman behind the desk was beautiful, and her clothes were obviously expensive. Maggie had expected all of that. She hadn't expected to see the two babies in matching jumpers crawling around the floor.

"Ms. Eagle Heart, I'm Rosebud Armstrong." They shook hands, and she turned to her receptionist. "Clark, can you handle the boys?"

"Can do. Come on, big guys. Let's go crawl on the rug!"

Ms. Armstrong gave Maggie an apologetic look. "It's

okay," Maggie said. "I like kids." Which was somewhat true. She did like kids. They just scared the hell out of her.

Clark scooped up both babies and managed to shut the door behind him.

"Thank you," Ms. Armstrong said. "I don't usually have Tanner and Lewis with me, but our sitter had an emergency today."

"How old are they?" For some reason, Maggie felt more comfortable making small talk with this woman than she had with anyone in a long time. Maybe it was that they were physically similar—light brown skin, dark brown eyes and long black hair. Sure, Ms. Armstrong's trousers and silk top made Maggie's skirt look shabby, but she got the feeling that Ms. Armstrong wasn't looking down her nose at Maggie.

"Eleven months. But enough about them," she added. "It's so nice to meet you. It's not often I get calls from both Yellow Bird and Carlson about the same woman."

Maggie's face flushed hot. "Is that bad?"

"It's interesting, more than anything." Ms. Armstrong looked Maggie over with a calculating eye. "Not too many people are capable of confounding one of them, much less both of them."

"Ms. Armstrong—"

"Please. Call me Rosebud."

"Okay. Rosebud. I'm not trying to confound anyone."

"That's what makes it so interesting." Rosebud continued to study her.

Maggie decided maybe she didn't feel so comfortable making small talk. She decided to try taking over the conversation. "Tommy said you'd gone to school with Mr. Carlson." Just saying his name out loud made her think back to the sight of him standing in her garden, looking happy to see her. Maybe she could get some answers on what kind of man James was.

"Did he, now?" A small grin flashed across Rosebud's face, but it was gone before Maggie could figure out what it meant. "That's true. He was top of the class. He's a damn good lawyer." She added, "Agent Yellow Bird mentioned that he told you a few things about how James operates."

"He just said Mr. Carlson likes to have insurance policies." Tommy hadn't mentioned anything about generous gifts or hot touches, though. Maybe that wasn't how James normally operated.

"That's correct. When James promises that he won't use your deposition unless he has to, I can personally guarantee that he *will* keep that promise. He will only use your information if the rest of his case falls apart. A worst-case scenario, if you will."

A lawyer who kept his promises? Rosebud seemed nice and all, but how could Maggie take the word of one lawyer about another? "Will that happen?" She'd had enough worst-case scenarios to last her the rest of her life. "Tommy said he's never lost a case."

"It's possible, but not probable." A sad sort of smile pulled at the corners of Rosebud's mouth. "He's never cashed in a policy, so you should be safe. He's offering you quite a deal in return for your information. Expunging a record isn't something done every day, you know, and relocation would cost him thousands."

"I wasn't sure." About anything. More to the point, she wasn't sure if she should want what she wanted, because she wanted to see James again. But seeing him again would mean telling him about what happened all those years ago, and if that happened, he'd see exactly how much of a nobody she was.

Rosebud didn't seem upset by that answer. Instead, she nodded and smiled. "Is there something else you wanted from James? Something he didn't offer?"

The way she asked the question put Maggie on edge. "Why? What did he say?"

There it was again, that smile that was too quick for her to interpret. "It's safe to say that he's not trying to screw you over. His morals are surprisingly well grounded for a lawyer. He did mention that he botched your first meeting badly, and he was trying to make up for that."

A special prosecutor would tell another lawyer he'd messed up? A new idea occurred to Maggie. James had said he'd picked up on the Lakota tradition of gifts "along the way." Rosebud Armstrong was a Lakota. "How well do you know him?"

"We've been friends for a long time." Her gaze didn't waver. "For a man of his station and aspirations in life, James has a unique talent. He is singularly able to see a person as they really are—not as they were or as they should be, and not as everyone else sees them. He judges a person on who he—or she—truly is." She got a wistful look on her face, as if she was seeing things that had happened a long time ago. "I think you can understand how hard it was to be the only Indian in law school, and a woman at that. But James never saw me in those terms. And in return, all he asked was not to be judged as the scion of the Carlson dynasty. That's why he's out here, scraping by as a prosecutor instead of being a lobbyist in D.C. Everything he has, he has earned."

While Maggie tried to guess what *scion* meant, she realized something. It sure sounded like Rosebud was talking around something, and that something sure seemed to be that maybe, just maybe, she and James had dated. Maybe he liked Indian women, Maggie thought. Suddenly, the prospect that he liked *her* seemed more plausible, less daydreamy.

Maggie chewed on all of that information. For so long, her life had been quiet and predictable. She beaded shirts and quilled moccasins and planted gardens and baked muffins.

Every Thursday, she went to the post office in Aberdeen. She watched silly TV shows and drank tea.

Now James Carlson was in her life, whether she wanted him there or not. She thought back to how he'd looked at her, with that strange mix of desire and respect. Did he see her for what she was? Was it possible for someone to know about her past and not sit in judgment?

Was it possible he was interested in her?

Rosebud interrupted her thoughts. "So what I'd like now is for you to tell me the whole truth, and nothing but the truth. James thinks he knows what happened a long time ago, but he wasn't there, and neither was I. Before I advise you as your lawyer, I have to know everything." Rosebud got out a recorder and turned it on.

Maggie told her everything. Her life's story took three hours and two pots of coffee.

James's phone buzzed to life on his desk. Rosebud's number. "What did she say? Is she okay?"

Rosebud sighed heavily. "I'm fine, thanks for asking. And the boys are great, but they miss Dan. He'll be back from Texas this weekend, though."

James rolled his eyes, grateful she couldn't see him do it. "Business first. How is Maggie doing?"

Maybe he was imagining things, but he swore he heard Rosebud smile. "She'll do it—on one condition."

"I already laid my cards out on the table. What else could she possibly want?"

Rosebud chuckled. "If I didn't know any better, I'd say you're crushing on her."

"Get real. She's a witness." His defense mechanism was hardwired. At this point, Rosebud could have accused him of being white, and he still would have flatly denied it. Besides, *crush* was such a juvenile term. James would prefer to think of it as being attracted to Maggie. Because, after spending more time in her company, he was *definitely* attracted to her.

"I know you, James. It's unlike you to not play close to the vest—unless you've got a vested interest in the outcome."

This was exhibit A of why a lawyer should avoid working with an old lover. There were no secrets. "Have you considered the possibility that I'm concerned for her well-being?" That was a completely honest reason that had nothing to do with the way he'd let himself touch her on the shoulder. Even that small touch had left him humming the whole drive home.

Again with the knowing chuckling. "That is the *only* possibility, my friend."

James debated hanging up on her, but that would only make the situation worse. He decided to redirect. "What does she want?"

"I'll let you off easy—this time. But don't think I'm going to let this drop. She also wants the record of Nanette Lincoln expunged."

"What?" Or, more specifically, *who?* Maggie had introduced the older woman as Nanette Brown.

"Look it up. You always do." Now Rosebud was teasing him. "Are we still on for dinner next Sunday?"

This was his one chance to get back at her. "As long as your housekeeper is doing the cooking—not you."

"So crushing." She giggled like a preteen girl. He half expected her to break into the *"K-I-S-S-I-N-G"* song from his playground days. "You're welcome to bring a guest, you know. And get back to me on that."

What, was she suggesting he bring Maggie as a date? That would be a clear violation of the rules, and there was no way James was going to make such a rookie, public mistake. He couldn't imagine a quicker way to derail all he had worked for.

Business first. He had to remember that. *Nanette Lincoln.*

He scrawled out the name as he hung up the phone and then stared at it. There was only one possibility, really.

Maggie Eagle Heart wasn't the only reformed criminal living in that house.

James pulled into an empty spot in front of Rosebud's office. Next to Rosebud's Audi was a Jeep wagon covered with equal parts rust and mud. Maggie was here. He tried to tell himself that he was only excited because this was another piece of his case. But what was the point of lying? He was looking forward to seeing her again. The two weeks since he'd been out to her house had seemed longer than normal.

Clark was waiting with a cup of coffee. "You can go into the conference room, Mr. Carlson. The court reporter is here. They'll be in momentarily."

James took his seat at the base of the table and got focused. He had a job to do today, and that job was getting a complete deposition from Maggie Eagle Heart. Nothing more and nothing less.

The door swung open, and Rosebud stepped into the room. "Morning, James," she said with a smile that verged on coy. Before James could process what that smile could mean, Rosebud stepped to the side and Maggie entered the room.

For one excruciating second, James forgot how to breathe. He'd seen her looking sweetly pretty and covered in grime. He'd liked her both ways, but he'd never dreamed she could be this stunning.

She wore a cream-colored suit with silky piping and a ruffle at the bottom of the jacket. The skirt was pencil thin, clinging to her hips like an old lover. Her toes—with nails painted a siren-red—were peeping out of soft pink shoes that matched the top underneath the jacket. Her hair was sleek and smooth, not a wisp out of place, and her makeup was ready-for-a-close-up done. Someone had spent a lot of time polishing this woman.

He shot a confused look at Rosebud, who gave him a professional smirk. She'd done this to torture him. Damn it. Because suddenly Maggie Eagle Heart didn't just look like a woman. She looked like a woman who could take him on—or bring him down. He wasn't sure if there was a difference right now.

Maggie looked at him from underneath heavy eyelashes. When she saw the look on his face, her eyes got wider.

"Mr. Carlson, glad you could join us today." Thank God Rosebud was able to focus. Someone had to be the grown-up in the room. "Shall we get going?" At the words, the court reporter's fingers were flying.

The next hour and a half were the worst in his life as he listened to Maggie recount each and every time she'd been hauled off in cuffs and brought before Maynard's court. The first time, Maynard had just demanded oral sex. After that, Maynard's demands had grown more depraved, and every time, Maggie had capitulated. With each retelling, James grew more enraged. He found himself wanting to protect her—even though he never let himself get emotionally involved in a case. Witnesses were just that—witnesses. But as he sat here and listened to Maggie's story, he wanted to do everything in his power to make sure no one would ever use her like that again.

Finally, they made it to the last encounter. For the first time all day, James truly didn't know the answer to the next question. What had changed? What had prompted Maggie to leave?

"I couldn't take it anymore," she said. "What kind of life did I have? I couldn't go home. I couldn't go back to Low Dog. I couldn't…" Her voice trailed off. "I couldn't live anymore."

"You attempted suicide?"

"Not consciously. When I left the courthouse that last time, I stole a car and drove. After a while, it started to snow. I'd driven off into a blizzard. No one knew where I was. I'm sure nobody cared. I kept driving until the car slid off the road and got stuck in a drift. I didn't know where I was, but it didn't matter. I got out of the car and started to walk."

"In the middle of a blizzard?"

"Like I said—I wasn't aware of what I was doing. It was cold, but the cold felt…good, you know? The pain was something real, something that I could say was honest and true." Her voice grew distant, as if she wasn't in Rosebud's office anymore, but was back out in the middle of a blizzard. "The cold was going to kill me, and it didn't want anything in return. It couldn't hurt me again and again. Just…slip off into the snow, and it was all over."

"Except it wasn't." They were done. This part held no relevance to his case. But he had to know.

"I saw a white light, and I knew I was dead. Except I still hurt. I didn't want to go to all the trouble of dying if it was still going to hurt. Then the snow changed. It solidified, and took on a shape. I thought it was Iktomi, the trickster spider from Lakota mythology, but it wasn't."

"Nanette Brown."

"Yes." Maggie's face brightened. Suddenly, she looked more like herself. "She said the spirits had told her I was out there, so she came looking for me. I had gotten really close to her house without knowing it. She'd tied a rope around her waist and to the house and come looking for me. She took me in. She helped me get clean, taught me how to bead and quill, gave me a life. *My* life."

That's why Maggie had wanted Nanette Lincoln's record expunged. She owed the older woman.

To think, when James had called up Nanette Lincoln's file and seen that she was wanted in a bank robbery in the late sixties, he'd seriously considered not agreeing to the condition. Now, instead of wanting to arrest Nan, he wanted to hug her. So she'd been in with a revolutionary crowd back in the turbulent sixties. She'd started over and redeemed herself by giving Maggie the same chance.

His admiration for Maggie grew. She'd not only survived, but she'd thrived. James had seen people—men and women— who let one bad relationship, one bad job, one mistake drag them down. Not Maggie. She'd come through the fires of hell a stronger, better woman. James had never been tested like that—would he be able to weather the storm and come out on the other side a better person? He wasn't sure. The only tragedy in his life was being the son of his parents, and that had left enough scars.

The deposition took almost two hours. Maggie looked drained but relieved. She smiled up at him when he stood, and he was surprised to see that she looked grateful. She didn't seem to hate him for making her relive those horrors. That didn't make any sense to him. He came from a world where people nursed grudges and exacted revenge years after the fact. No one in D.C. ever forgave and forgot.

But then, no one in D.C. ever seemed to have this much purity, this much peace. How was it possible? How could she have risen above the horrors of her past? There was only one possible conclusion. Maggie Eagle Heart was the strongest person he had ever met. Stronger than he was. He'd lived a clean, careful life, all in preparation for the presidency, but he couldn't claim the moral high ground that she could.

It was six in the evening now. He wasn't hungry, but he could tell that if he didn't eat something soon, he'd crash.

"We should get some dinner," Rosebud said, clearly reading his mind. "My treat."

"I should get home…" Maggie stood and smoothed out the cream skirt. "It's sort of a long drive."

"You need to eat. James, you in?"

"Only if Maggie is comfortable with that. We won't talk business." *Be comfortable,* he thought. He didn't want her to associate him only with a day of hellacious testimony. He wanted to give her something good to remember him by— even if it was just dinner. Dinner could be good.

As long as he didn't cross any line, that was.

"Then it's settled," Rosebud announced into the silence, blatantly denying the reality that nothing had been settled. "Chinese or Italian?"

Maggie grinned, her pink lips twisting off to one side. "I do like General Tso's chicken…"

"Done. Yu's it is."

Five

Maggie brought up the end of their little caravan as they pulled into a run-down strip mall about a mile from the court buildings. Rosebud's elegant sedan and James's expensive SUV looked grossly out of place, but at least her Jeep fit in.

This dinner thing was a mistake. She knew it, but here she was anyway. She should not be doing anything even remotely social with James Carlson. Even if she ignored the fact that she was horribly out of practice at small talk with people in general and men in specific, she couldn't forget everything that he now knew.

That wasn't all she couldn't forget. She didn't think she'd ever forget the look of anger on his face as she'd told her story. Maybe he'd been having semiharmless fantasies about slumming with someone so beneath him. Maybe he'd thought she was cute. Maybe he was into Native American women—she'd put money on him and Rosebud having been involved. None of that mattered because everything had changed.

If the Dishonorable Maynard had been in the room during the deposition, Maggie was pretty sure that James would have killed him. *For* her.

Her head was spinning, even though the car was no longer moving. In such a short time, her world had not just been turned upside down, but had also been knocked into a different orbit. Nan had been the only person to ever do anything for her—but suddenly, she had Tommy telling her he'd locked Low Dog up *for her*, and Rosebud getting Nan's ancient record cleared and buying expensive suits and paying for manicures *for her*.

What would James Carlson do for her? He'd already cleared two records and promised to keep Low Dog at a distance forever and ever—but that was before he knew everything. She'd expected the deposition to make her feel like the nothing she'd once been, but instead, a weird lightness made her want to smile. She had nothing left to hide now, she realized. In a strange way, saying the words out loud was almost freeing. She didn't have to pretend to be someone else anymore.

But the question was, how would James Carlson treat her now?

This whole situation would be easier to deal with if the man wasn't so attractive. Maggie sat in her car and watched him through the windshield. This was a different suit, a charcoal-gray with a faint pinstripe. She wasn't sure, but it might fit him even better than the first one she'd seen him in. She didn't know suits could look that good on a man, but his did. Not for the first time, she caught herself wondering what he looked like without all the fancy wrapping. He was only a few inches taller than she was, solid and fit. He would be something amazing.

Maybe he wouldn't look down on her now that he knew the truth. He hadn't during the deposition. If anything, he'd looked angry on her behalf. As if he cared about what happened to her, if that was even possible. Men like James Carlson didn't care about women like Maggie.

With a warm smile that spoke of his deep affection for his friend, he opened Rosebud's door with a gallant flourish. The two of them laughed, and a small part of Maggie hurt. Even in the waning light, James's smile was bright.

She had history with Tommy, but he wasn't the kind of man who laughed often. Laughing with Nan at their silly TV shows wasn't the same.

Wow. She couldn't tell if she was lonely or jealous or what, but it wasn't good. She should bail. Dinner was the worst idea possible.

Except it was too late. James turned and headed to where she was still sitting in her Jeep.

"Allow me," he said with a bow as he opened her door.

What the hell. If she was here, she might as well have a little well-deserved fun. She bit back a giggle. "Such chivalry!"

"One should always be chivalrous when one is in the company of a lady. May I?" Still bent over at the waist, he held out his hand and looked at her, a grin that bordered on goofy plastered on his face. He was waiting on her.

She hesitated. When she did, all the goofy disappeared right out of him. "Please, Maggie."

"Not too many people accuse me of being a lady." Why had she said that? Was she trying to make herself look stupid? Boy, she *was* out of practice.

"I'd like to think I'm not like too many people." He moved his hand a few inches closer. "This is just dinner with some friends."

When he put it like that… "Friends?"

"Friends."

She took his hand and swung her legs out of the car. His

hand was warm and firm against hers. *Strong.* Why on earth did that make her feel so weak?

He held on to her as she stood, as if he understood she wasn't used to heels this high. As soon as she was balanced, he let go of her hand—and then offered her his arm. "Shall we?"

Oh. My. A lawyer *and* a gentleman. Did such things exist? As they crossed the parking lot, they saw that Rosebud was on her phone.

"What's wrong?" James's arm tensed under her hand, and then he stepped away from her. "What's the matter?"

Rosebud held up a finger. "Are you taking him to the hospital? Why the hell not?"

"What?" James stood right next to Rosebud. Strong, Maggie thought again. Someone who was there for his friends.

"Lewis ran into the table and cut his head. He's bleeding like a stuck pig." Rosebud turned her attention back to the phone. "How do you know he'll be fine? Dan, I'm *not* kidding. Take him to the emergency room. I'll meet you there. Yes. Okay. Love you, too. Bye." She snapped the phone shut and headed for her car.

"Head wounds bleed a lot," James called after her. "He'll be fine."

"Thanks." Rosebud didn't sound as though she believed him. "Sorry about dinner. You two enjoy. Bye!"

Maggie watched Rosebud drive off, her stomach doing disorganized backflips. Just like that, she was all by herself with James at a restaurant. She wanted to believe he was the kind of man she could trust. But she couldn't. "Maybe we should call it a night."

"Are you kidding? If Rosebud finds out I let you drive home on an empty stomach, she'll rake me over the coals. Hell, Nan would chew me out." He sounded lighthearted, but there was no mistaking the intent in his eyes. "I'm buying you dinner, and that's final."

"Nan's not home tonight. She has bridge club." The moment she let that little nugget slip, she wished she hadn't. That was the last possible excuse she could have hidden behind.

"Dinner it is, then." He opened the door for her. She had no choice but to go on in.

The restaurant's eight booths were a red, white and blue plastic that had gotten cracked and torn in the thirty or forty years they'd been bolted to the walls. Only one other table was occupied, seemingly by the employees of the place. The floors and walls were grimy without being dirty, and each of the tabletops was completely bare—not even salt and pepper shakers.

She felt way overdressed for the place. She would have been happier in jeans and a T-shirt, but James didn't seem to mind. He greeted an older Chinese lady by name and slid into a booth in the middle of the restaurant. "Min, we'll start with the crab rangoon and spring rolls. The lady will have General Tso's chicken, and I'll have the usual."

The little woman nodded and smiled at Maggie before she tottered off to the back and yelled out things in Chinese.

He'd remembered what she'd said. She'd be lying if she said she wasn't flattered. "You come here a lot?"

He nodded, perfectly at ease. He had one arm draped over the back of the booth, and his tie was loose. He fit in everywhere—this mom-and-pop restaurant, his cramped office, Rosebud's spacious one, even in her tiny kitchen. He belonged everywhere, and she didn't fit anywhere. "I don't cook. I can say without reservation that this is the best Chinese joint in South Dakota."

"What's the usual?" Small talk. She could do this.

His smile was the easy kind. "Pork short ribs. Min knows how I like them."

"How long have you been in South Dakota?" After all, if they were going to make small talk, they might as well talk about him. What else could he possibly want to know about her? They'd covered all the messy stuff—which was everything.

"Two years. I go back to D.C. every couple of months."

"To see your parents?"

"My boss—Attorney General Lenon—likes to get face-to-face reports." He said this as if it was an everyday thing.

She got starstruck. "You're going to be president one day, aren't you?"

His smile got a little less honest, a little more phony-politician. She half expected him to shake her hand and find a baby to kiss. "That's the plan. It's what I was raised to be—the family business, if you will. I wouldn't be surprised if my parents had Carlson for President signs stockpiled in the carriage house."

"Is that what you want?" She had no business asking, but she wanted to know.

"That's the plan," he said as if that answered the question when, instead, it completely sidestepped it.

Lawyers, Maggie thought. Not to be trusted. No matter how good-looking, kind or generous they were.

Dinner arrived, and as they dug in, James went on, "The Kennedys were senators, attorneys general and presidents. The Bushes sent their sons to Colorado, Florida and Texas with orders to get elected governor and position themselves for national runs. W. was the big winner of that race. This is a tried-and-true formula. Sadly, I don't have any brothers to help improve the odds of a Carlson as president. It's all me."

"That's a lot of pressure on you."

At that, James tensed, the chopsticks halfway to his mouth. "I can handle it. It's all about who you know and not screwing up."

Maggie didn't know what to say to that. She didn't know anyone, but she had the screwing-up thing down pat. James could give her goofy smiles and buy her dinner, but the gulf between them was too huge to cross—even for daydreaming. She might not be the smartest girl in the world, but even she knew that a future president didn't like, kiss or—heaven forbid—fall for an ex-hooker. To do so would be screwing up in the worst way possible.

But then he looked up at her and gave her the kind of smile that made her heart do a hop, skip and jump all at once. "This is nice, isn't it?"

What was nice? "How do you mean?"

"Usually, when people realize who I am, they start working the angle—if I'm going to run for president, they need to get me on their side as soon as possible so I'll push for more guns or less guns or more spending or less spending or…" He sat back and exhaled. For the first time, she saw a crack in his armor. He could say he could handle the pressure, but she had to wonder if he was being honest.

Of course not, she reminded herself. Lawyers, by definition, were not honest men.

"You name it," he went on. "Everybody knows someone who wants something. Everyone has an agenda. Except you. You're different."

Maggie's heart went from skipping and jumping to flat-out cartwheels. On a deeper level, she understood exactly what he was talking about. Before, people had looked at her and never seen Maggie the person. Instead, she'd always been this *thing* to be used, abused and cast aside. She'd only been worth what people were willing to pay. That seemed to be what James was saying. People didn't want him—only what he could do for them. That was a hard way to live.

Min walked quietly up to the table and slipped the bill and two fortune cookies onto the table. As he fished out two twenties and handed them to the woman, Maggie picked one cookie up, weighing the easy promise of a better future in convenient dessert form. She handed it to him.

He cracked open his cookie and read the slip. "'Happiness is next to you.'" He mouthed something—maybe two short words.

"What?"

Their eyes met, and Maggie swore she felt a spark of electricity zing between them. "Nothing." That was what his mouth said, but his eyes were telling a different tale, one of desire. Did he want her even after hearing her story? "What does yours say?"

"'A great pleasure in life is doing what others say you can't.'" Her face started to heat up, and suddenly, she realized what he'd said to himself—*in bed*. She wished she'd saved hers for later, when she was alone. "I think I got your fortune."

She looked up and saw that he was watching her. The intensity in his eyes was unsettling. "Maybe I got the fortune I was supposed to get."

She remembered something Rosebud had said. James's great gift was seeing people as they were, not as they had been or were supposed to be. Maybe that's all he really wanted, the same common courtesy.

"Your father—he was a secretary of defense, right?"

"Yup. And my mother has family money dating back centuries." He rolled his eyes, as if this was embarrassing.

She couldn't resist needling him. It felt good to have a little power, to be in control of a conversation for once. "You must be *really* rich."

"Not me. My family."

"What's the difference?"

"I don't have much money. Most of it is in a trust until I get married." She must have given him a stunned look, because he added, "Really. I have to get married first. My mother has picked out my future first lady. Then I get the money to fund my campaigns. That's the plan."

"Says who?"

"My grandfather, in his will."

"That sucks."

He managed an amused grin. "It's not that unusual. Not in my world."

Maybe this was the world she saw depicted in all those reality-TV shows. James was living in some weird Real Political Dynasties of D.C.–world. "You have to get married to get your inheritance?"

"Correct."

"And you haven't married the woman your parents picked yet."

"I've been building my career." Then he exhaled again. Was this another crack in his presidential armor? "Pauline is a lovely woman, but…"

But what? Then Maggie realized what the *but* was—the angle. Everyone in his world was working one—and that most likely included future First Ladies. "If you don't marry her, you get nothing."

"You have a firm grasp on the situation."

"So don't marry her. There are worse things in the world than being poor. My family lived on a few thousand of welfare while I was growing up." The moment the words left her mouth, she felt stupid. Who was she to be offering advice to a future president of the whole freaking country? He probably had professional advisers he paid to tell him what he should and should not do.

"Never had a better offer." His plastic smile was back—not a crack to be seen in his armor right now. The man sitting across from her at this exact moment was presidential material, plain and simple.

"What about Rosebud?" Maggie was on thin ice here, and she knew it.

He shrugged. "She held out for a better man."

"Better than you?"

She shouldn't have said that, because James's eyebrows jumped up as he looked at her. Then his eyes drifted down to her lips, then over the expensive suit Rosebud had picked out for her. "You think I'm a good man?"

Oh, the ice she was on was so thin as to be nonexistent. Maggie realized she was wrapping her fortune around and around her fingers. She had to choose her words carefully here. She couldn't leave herself open. "We're friends. You said so yourself."

He leaned back, folding his hands together on the tabletop. "That's true. It would be highly unethical of me to act on an attraction to a witness. It could result in that witness's compromised testimony being thrown out of court and the attorney being disbarred."

That's what he said, but what she heard was, "I'm interested in you." Suddenly, she was having trouble breathing and her heart was doing cartwheels. "That would be bad, right?"

"It would end a political career, true." But the way he looked at her said, not so bad—might even be good.

She wanted it to be good. A part of her, a part that she'd locked away, was screaming for something that might be *good*. She wanted him, in a way that involved little clothing and even less talking. With everything he was and everything she wasn't, she still wanted him. And given the way he was looking at her—that respect mixed with desire, and a little hope thrown in for good measure—made it perfectly clear he wanted the same thing.

And the problem with that was… Oh. Right. She was a poor Indian woman with a messy history, living with a wanted fugitive, and he was—well, everything Tommy had said. Blue

blood, East Coast, rich. He said he played by the rules—
but did he? Or did he do whatever he wanted and justify it
later? Was he really different, or was he like that dishonorable judge?

"What are you going to do, James?" She braced herself for
some load-of-crap answer, the kind designed to make her feel
sorry for him—sorry enough to sleep with him.

"I'm going to win this case, get married and run for office. That's the plan."

"Plans can change, but only if you want them to."

He regarded her for several seconds, and Maggie was
afraid she'd crossed some line. "What I want is to do the
right thing. I always do." And then, as if he had to prove it to
her, he stood and offered her his arm again, ever the gentleman. "Let me walk you to your car."

As they headed for the door, he called out to the little old
lady his thanks for another wonderful meal, and then they
were outside, safely on the sidewalk. Clear, crisp air—the
smell of a South Dakota night in the early summer—cleared
her head. What was the "right" thing here? Was it right to
like him? To want him to like her? To imagine what it would
be like to kiss him? Was it right to want to see him again—
without testimony or lawyers, without messy histories or future campaigns involved? Was it right to want those things
without any other expectations?

At this exact moment, the right thing to do was to be polite. "Thank you for dinner."

"Thank you for joining me."

They walked toward the car side by side without touching. If he was so concerned with doing the right thing, he
wouldn't see her again—would he? "Will you need to interview me again?"

He didn't answer until they reached her Jeep. Maggie was
between him and her door. Suddenly, the space felt small.

James turned to face her, his body close enough to touch. She could feel the electricity between them, carrying with it the promise of something good. Even though she knew she shouldn't trust him, she wished she was the kind of woman who would pull James down into a passionate embrace. And she wished James was the kind of man who didn't care about morals, because then he might kiss her back.

He looked into her eyes, his intent clear. But then he said, "Ethically, I would only be able to see you again if I needed a clarification," in the kind of voice that men used to seduce a woman.

He wanted to kiss her. She could tell. "What kind of clarification?" The dinner-with-a-friend kind or the bring-your-lawyer kind?

He held her gaze for a moment longer, then took a step back. The tension between them snapped like a rubber band. "I won't know until I need it."

What kind of answer was that? One that left her hanging and him with all the power. She had to admire him, though. Any other man would have not only kissed her, but tried to convince her that twenty minutes in the backseat was fine. Not him. Maybe she really could trust him.

"You know where I live."

"Indeed, I do." He opened the car door for her and waited until she was buckled in before he shut it.

The last she saw of him in her rearview mirror, he was staring up at the sky again.

She hadn't seen the last of James Carlson.

She gave him a week, eight days tops, before he showed up again.

This time, she promised herself she'd be ready for him.

Six

James parked next to the post office in Aberdeen and waited. Yellow Bird had told him that Maggie came into town every Thursday to mail out packages. James should have been in the office, working on his case, but he was too distracted to focus. And that distraction's name was Maggie Eagle Heart.

He could not get her out of his mind, which was an odd feeling. James had always been able to maintain a laserlike focus on his job, and his track record showed it. This frenetic feeling that had him checking his cell phone every five minutes to see if she'd called or texted was completely outside his realm of experience. It was almost a physical compulsion, and it left him feeling not quite in control of himself.

Not in control? That would certainly explain why he was stalking her in the middle of the workweek.

There was no way around the facts. He wanted to see Maggie. It was just that simple. And the fact that it really *was* that simple bothered him. He was accustomed to being in relationships that were complicated. Hell, complicated was a gross understatement. He'd come from a world where emotions—of any kind—were used against people. Falling in love had never been simple. Maybe that's why he'd rarely done it.

Not that he loved Maggie. He didn't. This was merely an infatuation run amok. But things were different out here. He didn't have to plan an end-run around his mother or gauge if his father would deem James's actions good for his career. No spies would report back to his parents. Agnes was the only person who knew where he was, and he trusted her implicitly. He was interested in Maggie. He wanted to see her. So he did. How easy was that?

He was playing with fire, of course. It was one thing to want to see her. As long as he kept it to himself, he could want that and so much more and it would never come back on him. It was another to want to spend time with her—the kind of time that built into a relationship. There could be no relationship, period. With her history, Maggie would automatically rule him out as president. The media and voters wouldn't see the upstanding citizen she'd become. No one would be able to get beyond her record. He could always try to bury it, but even though he'd cleared it from the system, someone would come out of the woodwork. Someone always did. Then everyone would know. And that would be the end.

But here he was anyway, wanting to see her and acting on that basic desire. Another few minutes ticked by until James couldn't stand it. How the hell did Yellow Bird do all-night stakeouts? James got out his phone and began working through his email, keeping one eye on the post office.

Ten minutes later, he heard the familiar sound of an old Jeep from about half a block away. Bingo. Maggie parked four spots from him. She got out of her car and went around to the trunk. She looked very much as she had that first time he'd seen her in his office—long skirt, sleeveless top, hair loose. He was again struck by her beauty—a natural, unforced thing. She wasn't the kind of woman who spent hours in the gym or the spa every day, like Pauline Walker. She wasn't the kind of woman who would berate her children for ruining her figure, like James's mother had.

Everything about her, from the way she walked to the way she tossed her hair over her shoulder, said that she was comfortable in her own skin.

Even at this distance, he could see that the stack of boxes went almost up to the ceiling of her Jeep. No way she'd be able to get all of that in by herself. James hopped out of his car. "Good morning, Maggie."

She let out a little squeak as she spun around, sending the box on the top of the stack flinging off into space. James grabbed the package before it hit the ground. "James! What are you doing here?"

That wasn't the most encouraging thing she could have said, but James was undaunted. "I had something I needed clarified."

A bright pink blush shot across her cheeks, lighting up her face. She held his gaze without backing down. She wasn't afraid of him, but she wasn't acting all high-and-mighty. Instead, she smiled. She took his breath away. "Oh? What?"

What he really wanted was to know if she'd be glad to see him. And he already had his answer. *Yes*. But he wasn't about to overplay his hand. "Here, let me help you."

She held back for a second before she placed the rest of her boxes in his arms. "Thanks." Between the two of them, they got all the packages carried in.

"Morning, Maggie," the middle-aged woman behind the counter said. "Missed you last week. Got a lot today?" she asked, eyeing James behind his stack of packages.

"Morning, Jemma. I had to do something last week." Maggie managed not to look at him, but he could see it was an effort. She cleared her throat. "How are the kids?"

The two women chatted while Jemma weighed the packages and slapped the appropriate stamps on them. James hung around in the background, taking notes. Maggie was friendly, but Jemma did most of the talking. The personal information Maggie did volunteer was more about Nan than about herself.

The whole thing took almost half an hour. James fell into step beside Maggie as she left. "You do this every week?"

"Unless it's snowing. Or I have someplace I have to be." She favored him with a glance out of the corner of her eye.

"What do you do next?"

"Is that what you needed clarified?"

"Not really." They were outside now, away from the prying ears of the postal service. He took a step closer to her.

Maggie rounded on him, her hands on her hips. She would have looked stern except for the playful smile on her lips. "I'll make a deal with you. You tell me *what* you need clarified, and I'll tell you what I do next."

That made him smile. "I wanted to ask you if you would be able to come down to the office next week." A look of panic crossed her face, so he hurried to add, "Not to testify. I have a list of other potential witnesses that Yellow Bird has been unable to locate. I was wondering if you would recognize any names, know anything about what happened to them." Which was an excuse, plain and simple. But it was possible that Maggie had information he needed. He was just following up on a lead.

"I don't know…"

"It's just one afternoon. I have openings on Tuesday or Friday, if either of those works for your schedule." Nan had bridge club on Tuesdays, if he recalled correctly. And Agnes worked a half day on Friday.

"Oh." A small smile brightened her face—cautious, but

still engaged. "But we're just friends, right?" Her tone made it clear that she'd caught on.

"Absolutely. And, as this is for the case, it would be unethical of me not to follow up on the lead. However," he said, clearing his throat, "if you'd prefer to decline further involvement, we can leave it at that."

Then he stood back and waited. There couldn't be a more complicated way of asking a woman out—he would know. He'd negotiated dates around corporate takeovers and international incidents. Those were the hazards of growing up with his parents. But this was different. These complications were entirely his own doing.

It didn't matter how much he wanted Maggie or how different she was from any other woman he'd ever known. He'd pushed this as far as he could while remaining under the umbrella of legal. Whatever she said would have to stand.

Integrity sucked sometimes.

She looked up at him through thick lashes. Her beauty hit him high in the chest, momentarily paralyzing his lungs. *Say yes,* he thought. One afternoon. Maybe nothing would happen, but maybe something would. He wanted to know what that something would be. He shouldn't want to know, but he did. He couldn't help himself.

"I can come in on Friday."

He couldn't fight the grin, and was rewarded with one of her sunny smiles. It lit up her whole face. He wanted to bask in that warmth, but he knew he couldn't push his luck any further. "I have to get going, but I'll see you then, around two?"

James's office seemed less intimidating today than it had a few weeks ago. The woman behind the desk looked up and greeted her with a friendly smile. "Ms. Eagle Heart, how are you today?"

A momentary spike of panic flooded Maggie's system.

Was she supposed to remember the secretary's name? And if so, what the hell was it? But then she remembered—she had presents. Chocolate chip cookies could smooth over any social bump. She'd brought two boxes for this very reason. She fished out the smaller package. "Fine, thank you. I brought cookies."

"Why, isn't that sweet of you!" As the secretary stood, Maggie finally saw where the nameplate was on the desk. Agnes. "Thank you so much!"

"Do I smell baked goods?" James appeared in the doorway behind Agnes. His gaze locked onto Maggie, and he gave her a smile that walked the not-so-fine line between warm-and-friendly and hot-and-heavy. His tie was loosened and his sleeves were cuffed at the elbows. Some combination of warmth and heat rushed down her back. That was all it took for her to realize she was glad she'd come.

"Cookies," she said, offering up the box. "I made them this morning."

For an agonizing second, James looked at her—the kind of look that made it clear that he'd been waiting all week for this exact moment. Maggie felt a flush creeping down her chest, and she regretted the low scoop neck on her top.

"Come on in," he said, stepping back so that she could enter the office. "Agnes, before you leave, could you get us some coffee to go with these?"

Agnes was leaving already? It was only two in the afternoon. On a Friday. The full weight of this fact and all assorted implications hit Maggie so hard she almost stumbled. She was going to be alone with James—no prying eyes, no listening ears. Just her and the man she was infatuated with. He'd set this up. He'd known they would be alone.

She shouldn't have trusted him.

James motioned for her to follow him into the office, where she found a stack of files and a list of names waiting for her.

The chair she was supposed to sit in was on the opposite side of the desk from where James's chair was. And just like that, she was confused again. He'd gone to great lengths to make sure they'd be completely alone—and he was still going to keep his hands to himself? What kind of game was he playing?

Part of her was relieved she wasn't going to have to deck him. But a different part of her was disappointed. Would one kiss be so wrong? How was it possible that she wanted him not to make a move while also desperately wanting him to make a move? She didn't know what the hell she wanted. When had that become such a problem?

James left the door open and came around the desk, passing close enough to her that she could pick up the smell of his aftershave. It was woodsy, which she found amusing. James didn't exactly strike her as an outdoorsy kind of fellow. She must have grinned at this thought because when James glanced up, he shot her a full-power smile and said, "Yes?"

Busted. Maggie scrambled to come up with something that was not as personal as aftershave. "I hope you like the cookies."

James cocked an eyebrow, and Maggie knew she wasn't fooling him. But he opened the box and took out one. "Still warm," he marveled before he ate it. His eyes fluttered closed as he chewed, pure bliss making him look dreamy and satisfied. *Very* satisfied. "These are the best damn chocolate chip cookies I've ever had."

There went her stupid blush again. "Thank you."

Agnes came back in with the coffee and wished them both a happy weekend. Then she was gone and it was just Maggie and James.

The whole time, Maggie was trying to figure out what she wanted. Did she want him to kiss her? Did she want more than that? At what point did they cross some invisible, compromising line?

She had no idea what came next, except the stack of files on the desk.

That was a safe enough place to start, she guessed.

James stood at the side of the desk, looking down at her. "I would like you to check the names on the list and then look at the mug shots to see if you recognize anyone." Then he sat down, looked at his computer and ate another cookie.

That said no kissing, loud and clear. So she picked up a file and flipped it over.

The time passed quickly. Every new file was a blast from the past. She didn't know any of the girls, but she recognized them all the same. Somewhere, in a file in this office, was a photograph of her that was almost the same as all the others—beaten, bruised, strung out, dead inside. She had once felt so hopeless, and yet she was still here. She finished her stack and sat back, rubbing her temples. Why was she different? Why had she been found, when most of these girls were lost forever?

"Are you okay?" She looked up to find James staring at her, the worry obvious in his eyes.

"This is…harder than I thought it would be." She was surprised to hear her voice catch.

Then a funny thing happened. What looked a hell of a lot like guilt washed over his face, and he was out of his chair. He shut the door behind her and then had her by the hand and was pulling her up. Before Maggie could process what was happening, James had her wrapped in a huge hug. She tensed at the suddenness of the full-body contact, but as soon as she realized that he wasn't pushing her back against the desk, she relaxed into his arms. As odd as it seemed, this was just a hug. Tears hovered at the edges of her eyes, but she didn't want to cry right now. She wasn't even sure why she was so upset.

She pressed her face into his shoulder and tried to think happy thoughts. Like the fact that James was here, and his woodsy aftershave was just right on his skin. His arms felt even stronger than she'd dreamed they would, one hand just above the curve of her backside, the other between her shoulder blades. That hand was rubbing in small, calming circles. She allowed herself to enjoy this moment. It might be the only one she got.

At some point—probably after only a few seconds, but it felt longer—the embrace changed. It went from comforting to something else. Instead of small circles, James's hand moved up and down her back. He buried his nose in her hair and inhaled deeply, as if he wanted to savor her.

Heaven help her, she wanted to be savored. But she couldn't have sex in a lawyer's office. She had to remember she wasn't that kind of woman anymore.

James leaned back, his gaze intent. "Better?" he murmured, brushing a strand of hair away from her forehead. He glanced down at her lips and then back to her eyes. But he still didn't kiss her.

She had no idea if she should be relieved or disappointed. "Yes." And no.

"This is the last time I'll ask you to go back to that time." His voice hummed from deep in his chest, and Maggie swore he was purring. "Thank you for trying." He pressed his lips against her forehead. Not a true kiss, but something that was tender and sweet and honest all the same.

All Maggie could do was stand there with her eyes closed and melt inside. This was the perfect middle ground between being kissed and not kissed. It was almost as if James knew exactly what she needed, even if she hadn't been all too sure about it herself.

The question now was, what else would he ask of her? They had to be *on* that invisible, compromising line. One wrong move—hell, even a right one—would push them over the edge.

James pulled back and looked her in the eyes. "Is it okay with you if I call you to give you the updates on the case?"

Huh? She blinked at him a few times.

"I want to keep the lines of communication open between us," James said, not even a little bit ruffled by her cluelessness. "I can't think of a single additional thing that I need clarified, but I'd like to keep you informed of what happens."

If she lived to be one hundred and two, she wouldn't get lawyers figured out. But she was pretty sure he wasn't going to cross that compromising line—even if he was going to run up and down alongside it.

She touched her hand to his cheek, and he leaned into it. "I want to hear from you, James. Call me."

He turned his face into her hand and kissed her palm at the same time that he dropped his arms from around her waist. The message was loud and clear. They were done—for now. "Trust me, I will."

Seven

Light flashed through the window and off the TV. For one terror-filled moment, Maggie froze. Nan was at her weekly bridge club, leaving Maggie alone. Maybe someone was lost on a Tuesday night. Yeah, that could be it.

Even remembering that James had promised she'd get advance warning if Low Dog got out, she grabbed the shotgun out of the umbrella rack and pulled the curtain away from the glass in the door. She couldn't see much in the dark, but she could see enough.

A big SUV was parked about twenty feet away, next to her garden. A man was leaning against the front of the vehicle. She could see his broad shoulders clothed in a bright white dress shirt. His arms were crossed. Then he rubbed his eyes.

Her heart began to race. James was here. And he was upset. Six days had passed since she'd last seen him, though she'd spoken to him every night on some pretext or another. Why hadn't he called? This wasn't good news, that much was obvious, but she couldn't deny she felt a little thrill of excitement at seeing him anyway. Maybe Low Dog was out, maybe it was something else. Whatever the bad news was, she knew he'd kept his promise. He was here for her.

Maggie tucked the shotgun back in between the umbrellas, careful not to bump it. When she flipped on the porch light and opened the door, he straightened up. Even at this distance, she could see the sorrow in his eyes. For a selfish second, she wished she had on something fancier than a plain black broomstick skirt and blue long-sleeved T-shirt—something he'd like.

"James? What is it?" She took a step toward him, holding out her hand.

"Maggie." He sounded as if he was choking on her name. "I shouldn't have come—but I had to see you."

Her bare feet carried her down off the porch, a few steps into the cool dirt—and a few steps closer to him. "What happened? Is it…?" She was afraid to ask if it was something with the case, but she didn't know what else would bring him out here.

"The case is fine. Your testimony is still sealed. No one has to know you're a part of it. I…" He cleared his throat and rubbed his eyes. "I had to talk to someone, and I can trust you."

He could? Part of her brain tried to tell her it could be a trick—he might be trying to manipulate her emotions. But it didn't feel that way. She went to him and looked up into his eyes. He was hurting.

She touched her hand to his cheek. His eyes squeezed shut and he took the kind of deep breath that meant he was choking down pain. She knew how that felt, too. "Come inside," she whispered, taking his hand. "Tell me what's happened."

His eyes still shut, he nodded and followed her into the

kitchen. He didn't let go of her hand, and she didn't let go of his.

Maggie's heart was pounding. This was dangerous, but for the life of her, she couldn't figure out if it was the good kind of danger or the bad. James's unscheduled arrival—on the night he had to remember Nan wasn't home—set off warning bells. But he wasn't making a move on her. She wanted to believe—desperately—that he really needed her.

When they got into the kitchen, Maggie released his hand and busied herself making tea. James leaned against the counter, arms crossed, his eyes unfocused. What he did next would tell her if he was a man she could believe in or not.

Making tea wasn't exactly a plan, but she made it work. She got the kettle on, the two nicest mugs out and scrounged up the few packets of fake sugar to display next to the sugar bowl. Maybe she should offer him something to eat? She was digging around in the fridge for the lemon pound cake she'd made yesterday when James cleared his throat. "When I was a kid, I didn't spend a lot of time with my parents. Dad was always working, and Mother…well, she was busy."

"Were you alone?" That didn't seem right. She'd been more or less abandoned, but surely rich people didn't do that to their kids.

"No. I had the same nanny from when I was two until I was eighteen. She raised me." His voice caught, and Maggie's heart broke a little bit.

She knew how this story ended. Something had happened to the nanny. "Tell me about her."

"Her name was Consuela. She was from Costa Rica. My mother hired her before Zoe Baird got her nomination for attorney general pulled for hiring illegal immigrants."

She hated to interrupt him, but… "Who?"

"Sorry. Back in 1993, a woman didn't get to be attorney general because she'd hired immigrants as nannies and chauffeurs without the proper paperwork. Of course, half of D.C. had undocumented aliens running their households and raising their children. I had Consuela."

"Oh." Nannies and chauffeurs. Attorneys general and future presidents. For a moment there, Maggie had felt close to him. Now the distance seemed gulf-size again. Their worlds were too different. He could trust her and she could like him, but when it came down to it, there was no way in hell she could do anything more than make him tea. She wasn't sure she should even be doing that.

"My father had started moving up the political food chain. I convinced him that we needed to make Consuela legal—green card, taxes, the whole thing. By the time Dad went before congressional committees, all he had to do was apologize for a hiring oversight."

"You were how old?"

James gave her a weak smile. "Ten, I think. I learned a lot about how the world worked then."

No wonder he was going to be president one day—he'd been outsmarting congressional committees since he was in middle school. But at this moment, he didn't seem like the leader of the free world. He seemed like a regular guy who'd lost someone important.

"She was this quiet, tiny woman with quick, black eyes. She'd never finished school in Costa Rica, but she helped me with all my homework." He brightened. "I used to joke with her that she should go up to get my high school diploma with me because she'd earned it, too. She drove me to all my games…" His brief joy faded as his voice caught.

"She sounds like a special woman."

"She died. Her heart gave out. Two weeks ago. I…" He looked up at her, his eyes wet. "I just found out today. I missed the funeral. I didn't get to say goodbye. And when I asked my mother why she didn't tell me, she said, 'It was *just* the nanny.'" His tone changed to something high and tight—and mocking. Anger flashed over his face, pushing back his sorrow. "Like she couldn't even be bothered. Consuela was more my mom than Mother was, and I…" Just as quick as it had come on, his fury dissolved.

"I'm sorry," Maggie said. She knew she shouldn't, but she went over to him and slid her arms around his waist. He had comforted her in his office without crossing the line—surely she could do the same? Besides, he'd said it himself—no one would ever know she'd testified. They were friends. Friends were there for each other.

James's chest shuddered as he drew in a breath, then he folded her into his arms and buried his head into her neck. "I didn't have to be anyone else with her. She didn't care if I became president or if I worked in a grocery store." His voice was a hoarse whisper. "She was proud of me, no matter what."

Maggie remembered what Rosebud had said—that James's great gift was to see people as they really were. "I like you just the way you are, James. I always have."

He pulled her in tighter, until the whole of her front was pressed against every inch of his. "I trust you, Maggie. I need you."

Maggie felt the span of muscles under his shirt. Instantly, she was aware of him in a new way, a way that sent nervous shivers up her arms and down her back. A strange tension coiled around her, not in her belly as if she was nervous, but lower and tighter.

She was no virgin, obviously. But these feelings—these sensations—they were new and more than a little overwhelming. In the best way.

She should let go of him this very instant. Right now. This was the moment when they either crossed the line or backed away from it.

But backing away would mean letting go of him, and letting go of him would most likely mean never having this moment again.

Maybe it was selfish, maybe it was just being there for a friend—maybe it was both. Whatever it was, Maggie didn't pull away. She couldn't, not when he needed her so much. Not when she needed him, too.

So she ran one of her hands up his back until her fingers tangled with his hair. He exhaled against her skin, the warmth sending another wave of shivers down lower. "I need you, too."

Dear God, had she really said that out loud? Part of her brain scrambled to slam on the brakes, but before she could change her mind, he pressed his lips against her neck. That single touch weakened her knees and her resolve.

Then James pulled back. For a searing second, he looked her in the eyes, and she saw the battle in his gaze. He slammed his lips into hers with an emotion that was both desperate and furious. His teeth clipped her upper lip, the pain in direct contrast to the sheer thrill of the thing. He was *kissing* her. He *liked* her. Part of her brain swooned. A kiss, a *real* kiss. Despite how rough it was, something in her quivered with need. He'd taken this kiss. She wanted him to take another.

Her mind and body wanted to give him that kiss, and maybe something more. To hell with being compromised.

Her thoughts made a jumble look calm and organized. Yeah, she'd wondered what sex would be like now, as Maggie Eagle Heart—what being loved would be like. It'd been so long, Maggie thought. What if she never got another chance? What if this was it?

Then he took that second kiss, pulling her body against his until she could feel more than the hard planes of his chest, and she lost the ability to think at all. His tongue thrust into her mouth, tangling with hers until she wasn't just quivering with need. She *shook* with it.

He took that as a yes. His hands slid down and cupped her bottom. He picked her up and spun her around until she was all but sitting on the counter.

"Oh, Maggie." His voice was something low and dangerous, but he didn't stop as he kissed her for the third time. This time, his lips moved over her chin, down her neck and then he pulled the V of her shirt away, revealing her basic white bra. That, too, was pulled aside, and she was exposed to him. His mouth closed around her nipple.

She couldn't help it. She leaned back and braced herself by wrapping her legs around his waist to give him more. He made a guttural noise in the back of his throat, and then her other breast was being sucked with that furious need. Between the feel of his mouth and her own intense desire, her nipples went rock hard.

His teeth scraped the sides of her breast as he jerked her skirt up. Then he undid his pants and pulled the crotch of her panties to one side. Then he was against her. Then he was in her.

The suddenness of the sensation drew a long, ragged gasp from her throat. Once James was deep inside her, he pulled her off the counter. His arms wrapped underneath her as he lowered her body more firmly onto his, and then he did the unexpected again. He kissed her. While they had sex.

And she liked it. Oh, Lord, she liked it. She forgot about what she'd been and what she was and let herself just *be* here with this man. He rocked his hips up and back as he lifted her up and down, using the counter to brace them both. The whole time, he kissed her lips, sucked on her tongue and kept repeating, "Oh, Maggie," over and over in that low, dangerous voice.

Her body responded. Heat rushed between her legs and surrounded him where their bodies met. With each thrust, tension tightened her thighs around his waist, her arms around his neck. *This* was what she wanted.

Her head fell back, and he fastened onto one of her breasts again. The intensity—that wasn't something she'd expected to feel. She'd expected the skin-on-skin contact, sure, but she hadn't thought it would make her blood pound so hard, make her want to cry out with aching desire. She hadn't known sex could feel this freeing. That she could like it this much.

Unexpectedly, the coiling tension that held her body tight around his snapped back on her. This time, she did cry out as the climax threw her forward. Only his body stopped her from falling to the floor.

Then, as suddenly as he'd entered her, he pulled out with a roar that was muffled by her hair. Moisture trickled down her legs.

So different was all she could think. *So good.* But the featherlight satisfaction of a long-awaited climax turned into a dead weight that pulled her down off her cloud. No condom. Oh, *no*.

She looked at James, who had apparently come to the same conclusion. "I, uh, I pulled out," he stuttered as he set her down.

Maggie rushed for the bathroom. Because her panties had stayed on, they'd taken the most direct hit, but paranoia had already set in. How could something that had felt so very right seem so terribly wrong just seconds later?

Not only could she not have a baby, she could *not* have James's baby. The future president *did* not have little bastards running around, especially not little bastards conceived with former hookers. It just wasn't *done*.

She sat on the toilet in a state of shock. All this time, she'd been deluding herself into thinking that she'd changed, that she'd become a responsible, trustworthy adult. But a responsible woman would have demanded safe sex. Hell, a responsible woman wouldn't have let James get to a point where he could be disbarred. She'd sunk them both, all because he trusted her and she liked him—all because she'd given in to all those new, different feelings.

She had to get it together. This situation was salvageable. No one else knew about their…contact. It was up to her to keep it that way. She could keep a secret, after all, and James, well—they could say this was privileged and he simply couldn't tell anyone else. She'd have to go back into town tomorrow and buy a stick to pee on. Or see if the pharmacy had those morning-after pills. Possibly both.

These thoughts calmed her. This situation was not hopeless. She had a plan. When she opened the bathroom door, she had what felt like a composed, cool look on her face. She'd had to leave her underwear in the bathroom hamper, but the skirt wasn't too bad. She could do this—pretend nothing had happened.

At least, she thought she could, until she saw him again. James was now sitting at the table, his head buried in his hands. He had his pants fixed, but he looked odd with his shirt untucked. He seemed even more upset than he had before.

Again, she was drawn to comfort him, but this time, she held back. No way in heck could she risk doing something stupid twice in a row. "The bathroom is at the end of the hall, if you need it."

He sucked in air as though he was drowning, but he didn't move. "I—I didn't come here to do that. That wasn't how I wanted it to go, not at all. Jesus, you must think I'm like… like Maynard."

"I don't." Which was the truth. What had just happened between them was kind of a mess, but she knew in her heart that he was *nothing* like Maynard.

She walked up behind him and put one hand on his shoulder. Immediately, he covered it with his, clinging to her fingers. "If—when—this happened, I wanted to make love to you the right way."

Make love. Her mind stuck on those two words like flies on flypaper. "But I'm just your witness."

He stilled for a moment, then stood, his hand never letting hers go. He turned around and kissed her. Not like before, oh, no. This time, his lips were soft and giving, saying what the words hadn't. *I promised,* they said. *And I meant it.* "No, you're not," he said in a quiet voice. "You're more to me than that." And he kissed her again.

This kiss left her a different kind of breathless. This wasn't a happening-too-fast feeling, but a happening-as-it-should feeling. Out of the babble of confusion in her head, one thought rose above the others. This was normal. Perfectly, wonderfully normal.

It didn't last. His phone rang.

Maggie jumped so hard she was amazed she hadn't busted anyone's lip. James hesitated, as if he didn't want to let go of her, but then he sighed and stepped away.

"Carlson," he said, sounding like a professional in every way and nothing like the man who'd been in her kitchen for the last fifteen minutes. "Yes. *What?*" The thunderous roar knocked Maggie backward until she bumped into the door frame. "He did *what?* Jesus Christ, does Lenon know? Yes, I know that's the only option. Oh, God. Okay. I'm, uh, I'm out of town at the moment. Two hours. Just patch him through."

He hung up and dropped his head, his shoulders slumping in utter defeat. "James?"

"That was Agnes. The judge in my case just handed down his ruling on admissible evidence. He ruled in favor of the defense." James's voice was flat and lifeless.

Maggie had been worried about him when he'd been upset, but this deadness? This scared her. "What does that mean?"

"He threw out my case—the wiretaps, the witnesses— gone. Just like that."

That part she understood. Plan A had failed. Which only left one option. Her. "Except for the insurance policy."

He looked at her, and she couldn't begin to make sense of the emotions churning beneath his worried brows. "Yes." Before he could say anything else, his phone rang again.

"Carlson. Yes, Mr. Lenon." His eyes flicked up to her face as the person on the other end shouted loud enough that Maggie could hear it, but not loud enough so that she could understand what he was saying. "Yes, sir. I'm aware of that. It's disappointing, I agree. But I have an insurance witness."

They were talking about her. Lenon? Maggie came up with nothing. The name sounded familiar, but...then it hit her. Todd Lenon. The attorney general of the United States.

Oh, no. The attorney general was talking—yelling—about *her.*

She covered her mouth with her hand, as though that would keep her heart from jumping all the way out of her chest. Margaret Touchette wasn't dead, after all. The bitch was alive, biding her time until she could wreak havoc on Maggie's life. Because that's exactly what would happen. A corruption trial was big news. People would find out who she was, what she'd done.

She'd have to take James up on his offer to relocate her, give her a new life. Everything she'd been here with Nan, everything she'd done for the last decade would be gone, lost in a courtroom. What would happen to her? What would happen to Nan?

James looked at her again, the wildness in his eyes seeming sadder this time. What would happen to James—the man who never lost a case? The man who always did the right thing?

She felt as lost as he looked. For some crazy reason, she still wanted to comfort him. Her life, and all her past mistakes, were about to become public record, but she wanted to tell *him* it would all be okay. He looked as if he needed to hear it.

"I'm apprising the witness of the situation now, sir." More shouting occurred. "Yes. Really?" This last word came out in a shocked tone, but seconds later, James had things back under control. "Of course. Friday at three. We'll be there." He hung up and dropped his eyes.

He couldn't even look at her. She wanted to ask *what* was going to happen on Friday at three, but nothing came out. Not even a squeak.

James flipped his phone over and a minikeyboard appeared. He tapped out a message faster than Maggie would have thought possible, all the while seemingly having forgotten that she was right there, too scared to move.

He tapped out another message—maybe the same one, she couldn't tell—and then looked at his phone as though it held all the answers. The seconds seemed impossibly long as he stared at the damn thing.

"Well?" she demanded, managing to sound stern.

"The attorney general wants to meet with me about my case. I have to present the remaining admissible evidence and convince him that I can still get a conviction."

That was a whole lot of "I" and not a lot of "we." Then she realized what he'd said—he had to present the remaining evidence. *She* was the remaining evidence. "I have to go to Washington?"

"On Friday." He said this in a no-big-deal tone of voice, but that worried, heartsick look was back in his eyes. He took two steps closer to her. "I'll be with you the whole time."

Was that supposed to be comforting after everything that had happened tonight? "Is Rosebud going?" Because meeting the attorney general for the whole freaking country sure *seemed* like a good time to have your lawyer handy.

"No. This isn't just your testimony anymore, Maggie. It's my case. You're my witness. As far as Lenon knows, you're a strung-out former hooker. I've got to prove to him that you're a reliable witness—someone the jury will believe. If you're not, he'll kill the case." The way he said it made it clear that the case wasn't the only thing Mr. Lenon would kill. Maggie could see James's career flashing before his eyes. And if his career went, where would that leave his grand political plans?

"But I—we—" Just had sex. Just compromised the witness. Just broke every rule in his book. Hell, in her book. She shouldn't have, but she looked down at her belly. One of her hands splayed out over the gentle swell of her stomach. She was his witness, but she was more than just that. What if she was pregnant?

"I know," he said, putting his hand on top of hers. Then he wrapped his other arm around her shoulders and hugged her. "If anything…happens, I'll take care of you. Whatever you want."

God, that sounded so good. She hadn't realized *that* was what she needed to hear until she heard it. Part of her wanted to shake it off—words were words, after all—but a bigger part of her wanted to believe him.

He cleared his throat. She could tell that the next thing he said was going to be all lawyerly just by the way he pursed his lips. "Something isn't right about this, Maggie, but I don't know what it is yet. I'll get Yellow Bird to start digging—if anyone could come up with something else I could use against Maynard, he could. We'll get this figured out. But until then…"

"We have to go to Washington together." She didn't know what to think, so she was sticking to the facts here.

"Yes."

She swallowed. "Will we have separate rooms?"

He hesitated, and then said, "Yes. It would probably be for

the best if we limited our personal involvement and kept…
tonight…to ourselves."

Yes, she thought. *It would probably be for the best if I
didn't get knocked up with an illegitimate child.* He kissed
her forehead. "This isn't how I wanted it to go, Maggie. I'll
work on a solution, I promise. But that doesn't change things.
I'm fond of you."

Fond. Such an odd word. Despite it all, she smiled at him.
"I'm fond of you, too." It didn't make any sense, but it didn't
have to. Not right now.

His phone rang again. With a final squeeze, James let go
of her.

He'd answered the phone when the front door slammed
open and Nan's breathless voice called out, "Maggie? Are you
okay?" seconds before she huffed her way around the corner.

She pulled up short when she saw James on the phone,
then gave Maggie a terrified look. But before Maggie could
even begin to explain what was going on, James hung up.

"Rosebud's going to call you in ten minutes. She'll walk
you through what's going to happen in D.C. to help you pre-
pare." He sounded so formal. James turned to Nan. "I need to
get back to the office, Ms. Brown. If you or Maggie have any
questions, please call me." Nan's open mouth snapped shut
and she managed a polite nod. James turned back to Maggie.
The look he gave her was almost as good as hugging her had
been. "We'll be leaving South Dakota early Friday morning.
My assistant will call you with the details. I'll see you then."
Without another word, he turned and let himself out.

"What the hell happened?" Nan shouted.

Maggie listened as the SUV pulled away. Only after the
crunch of tires on rock had faded did she turn to her fairy
godmother. "Well?" Nan demanded, tapping her foot.

She knew her dearest friend in the world was waiting, but
Maggie needed to get her thoughts in order. So she finished

making tea. As she poured the water, things began to crystal-lize. She couldn't tell Nan about the sex. If she wasn't preg-nant, then it would be as if it never happened. James couldn't afford to have anyone else know about the compromising position he'd had her in. She'd have to bury that memory—a sweet memory of freedom and fondness—deep. But not too deep. She'd need that to keep her warm on cold winter nights.

He'd needed her, but when it got down to brass tacks, he'd needed his case—his victory—more. He wasn't like May-nard. But she shouldn't have trusted him.

It was a mistake she wouldn't make again.

Finally, she sat, and Nan sat with her. They only had a few minutes before Rosebud called her. She'd have to talk fast. "Everything," she said simply.

Eight

Maggie pulled into a spot in front of Rosebud's office. The place looked deserted. She checked her watch—9:58 a.m. She was two minutes early. And she was flying to Washington, D.C., in twenty-one hours. With James Carlson. To meet the attorney general.

She sat in the car and rubbed her temples. Her head hurt, but that was probably the lack of sleep and the stress. Oh, this was a mess, as evidenced by the bag from Walgreens in the passenger seat. The paranoia had been thick at the store, so she'd gone ahead and bought the three-pack of pregnancy tests. She had that awful feeling that no matter what the first test said, she wouldn't believe it until she got at least two out of three similar answers. But she hadn't been able to bring herself to ask for the morning-after pill. She didn't know why.

She checked her watch again: 9:59. Time seemed to slow down when a girl hadn't slept. As the seconds did everything *but* tick by, she found herself looking at the Walgreens bag again and wondering. She'd never wanted kids. Kids scared her. She didn't have the first idea how to take care of a kid. Her own childhood had been hellacious, after all. The odds were better than good that she'd screw up a kid. She didn't want that on her conscience.

So why the hell was she sitting here hoping she was pregnant?

Stress and sleep deprivation. That had to be it. She must be borderline delusional.

She checked her watch a third time. Ten o'clock. And no sign of life in the office yet.

Maggie leaned her head back and let her eyelids close. Immediately, images of James popped up behind her lids. James, looking heartsick. James, kissing her with a vengeance. James, taking her in the kitchen. James, being fond of her. James, leaving.

Her mind began to drift in nonlinear patterns. What had he looked like as a kid? Had he worn suits to school? And what kind of parents decided their kid would be president come hell or high water, anyway? They weren't the Kennedys, were they? No, she remembered. They were a totally different dynastic family.

Luckily, a huge four-door truck pulled up next to her, saving her from her thoughts. Rosebud popped out of the passenger-side door and waved.

Maggie got out and locked her car. She turned back to Rosebud just in time to have a sleeping baby thrust into her arms. *Not helping.*

"Hold Lewis," Rosebud said as she reached back into the car. Maggie heard her say, "No, give me Tanner and you carry the suitcases, please and thank you, honey."

Lewis was a warm, heavy weight in Maggie's arms. She made the mistake of looking down at the boy, and that irritating desire to have a baby of her own—to have James's baby—got a little stronger. His eyebrows jumped with whatever dreams babies had. He looked so peaceful, so innocent—so *not* screwed up. Maggie leaned down and sniffed his head, the clean-baby smell hitting her so hard she almost staggered under the weight of it.

A tall, handsome man was hefting a third suitcase out of the truck bed. He paused long enough to tip his cowboy hat. "Howdy, Ms. Eagle Heart. Dan Armstrong. I'd shake your hand, but—" He broke out in a lopsided grin as he lifted all three pieces of luggage and nodded to the baby in her arms.

"Hi." Even in her exhausted state, she knew that if she was going to be meeting the attorney general, she'd need to do better than that. She cleared her throat and tried again. "Hello. It's nice to meet you, Mr. Armstrong."

His grin got bigger as he waited for her to go in front of him. Rosebud had already disappeared into the building, and lights were coming on. "You'll be fine. James will take good care of you. He's a good guy."

A complete stranger could tell how nervous she was? Man, she was *so* screwed. "Have you ever met Mr. Lenon?"

"Yup. He's a pompous, arrogant ass." Dan chuckled. "I'm not the sort of fellow to tell a stranger what to do, but *if* I were, I'd tell you to keep your chin up. D.C. is a snake pit. Most everyone there will step on whoever it takes to get a little closer to the top. Don't let yourself be a rung in their ladder."

Maggie looked at this Dan Armstrong. "What about James?" She had no business asking, but he was from D.C., after all.

"James?" Dan dropped the suitcases and held out his arms to take the baby from her. "Yeah, James is on a ladder. Maybe not the one he wants…" With that cryptic observation, Dan turned his attention to the baby.

In short order, Maggie found herself back in Rosebud's office, suitcases strewn everywhere. Rosebud wasn't meeting her eyes. Maybe it was just the paranoia, but Maggie got the feeling that either James had told her about the wild sex, or she'd figured it out. Maggie began to fidget. "It's a good thing you're about the same size I was before the twins came along," Rosebud said in an unnaturally light voice. Damn it, she knew about the sex. "If we had more time, I'd take you shopping again, but… Oh, that suitcase is all cocktail dresses."

"Really?" Maggie pulled out a little black dress with layers of ruffles going all the way down. Panic left a metallic taste in the back of her throat. "Why do I need a cocktail dress?"

"You're meeting Lenon at three on a Friday. He's notorious for being about an hour behind schedule, and then he'll have to have a little verbal sparring match with James. By the time you get out of there, it might be close to six, and he throws a cocktail party every Friday night. It's how he rewards people for pulling hundred-hour weeks."

"Seriously?" Was this her hard-earned tax dollars at work?

Rosebud nodded. "He's famous for them. It's a huge networking thing—you'd be surprised at who shows up. James will have to go, and if I know Lenon, he'll expect you to be there, too. He'll want to see how you handle yourself."

The metallic taste got stronger. Maggie fought back the gag. "I don't want to network. I don't want to go to D.C."

"Don't panic!" In a second, Rosebud had her by the arm and was leading her to the couch. "Sit down and put your head between your knees. Breathe, Maggie."

Breathing was easier said than done, but after a few minutes, the awful taste was less awful. "What the hell am I going to do?"

"You're going to stick close to James. You can do this, Maggie." Her arm still around Maggie's shoulder, Rosebud sighed. "Look, I'm going to be up front with you. Having his case thrown out has never happened to James before, and frankly, it's a little suspicious."

Maggie wished she understood this whole thing better. None of this was her world. "Like how?"

"This is a corruption trial. It may run deeper than James thought." Rosebud shook her head in disgust, and Maggie could see that she was tired of this fight. But then she perked back up. "What that means for you is that you can't announce you're a witness in D.C. You're the last line of defense for this case. James needs to keep you as safe as possible. Your testimony *cannot* be compromised. Yellow Bird might find something to keep you off the stand, but he was stretching it to find you."

There was that word again, *compromised.* Maggie couldn't look at Rosebud, so she stared at the clothes bursting out of the suitcases. Should she tell Rosebud that she'd already been compromised? That, for the first time in her life, and against her better judgment, she was falling in love—with the most inappropriate man possible?

Rosebud didn't seem to notice her silence. Maybe she hadn't guessed about the sex. Or she was willfully overlooking it. Either way, Maggie felt as if she was getting a pass. "If you find yourself talking to anyone outside of Lenon's office, you are the legal assistant of Rosebud Armstrong, attorney at law. Leave everything else open. If they ask where you went to school, change the subject. If they get obnoxious about it, leave. Spill a drink, step on a toe, accuse them of racism, whatever. It doesn't matter." She gave Maggie a serious look. "You *can* do this. I have complete faith in you." The conviction in her voice was both comforting and surprising.

Before Maggie could think much about it, Rosebud had pulled up a shimmery blue dress with fancy cap sleeves. "You'll need two suits and one cocktail dress." She handed Maggie the dress. "Let's get started, okay?"

Nine

James sat in his car, watching the trickle of traffic in the Pierre Regional Airport. Not much was happening at four-thirty in the morning. Next to nothing, in fact.

The two days since he'd seen Maggie had been some of the longest of his life. He and Agnes had been working around the clock to shore up his case. Lenon wanted this conviction as much as James did, but Lenon would kill the whole thing before he'd risk letting James make a fool out of the department. James had sent Yellow Bird back out to find something—anything—admissible on Maynard.

Anything that wouldn't put Maggie on the stand.

Another set of headlights flashed over the parking lot. Not a Jeep. Damn.

He would not sleep with her again. Not that they'd done any sleeping before, but she was off-limits. No one needed to know about the one-and-only time James had ever lost his head over a witness. It didn't matter that he was doing everything in his power to keep her out of the courtroom. It didn't matter if he was fond of her. What mattered was justice, putting Maynard away for good. That's what he had to remember. Which did not explain the pack of condoms he'd shoved into one of the inner pockets of his suitcase. He wondered how many times he'd have to tell himself this before it sank in through his thick skull.

Agnes had reserved a suite at the Watergate Hotel—a small apartment, really, with an office, dining room, kitchen and two separate bedrooms. There was nothing unusual about that. He'd shared suites with other sensitive witnesses who required constant monitoring. It was a lot like being in a hostel—suddenly, you had to share the coffeepot with someone who you'd rather not.

But this someone? A different story. A different someone.

Not sleeping with her, he said again as another set of headlights cut through the dark. This time, it was a Jeep. James grabbed his bag and went to meet her.

Be the professional, he told himself as he opened her door for her. "Good morning, Maggie."

The dome light cast long shadows over her face. He couldn't see her eyes, but he could see that she had on a pair of kitten heels and a tailored, chocolate-brown wool suit. Her hair was loose, and he didn't think she had on any makeup. Didn't matter. She was stunning, even more so given how damn early it was.

She gazed up at him. The air grew sharp between them, as if things were crystallizing right before his eyes. His pulse began to pick up speed. Despite *not* thinking about it, his mind went rushing back to the narrow confines of her kitchen and the warmth of her welcoming body.

James shook his head, chasing such forbidden thoughts away. He had to stay focused here. The lawyer part of his brain was ecstatic that she had, in fact, shown up. The rest of him was just ecstatic to see her again.

He thought he saw the corners of her lips curl up into a tentative smile. "Good morning, James."

He could only stare at her as she unfolded those legs from the car.

Not sleeping with her. Not even *thinking* about it.

She went back to the trunk and pulled out a nice overnight bag. Silently, they made their way inside the airport.

He kept an eye on her as they checked in and took their seats by the gate. The airport wasn't big by any stretch of the imagination, but James could tell by the way her eyes got wide as she looked around that she'd never been here. Then a new thought occurred to him. "Have you ever been on a plane?"

"No. I've never even left the state." Her voice was small, but still surprisingly professional. She was nervous, but doing an amazing job of hiding it.

"The first flight will be in a little puddle-jumper." He tried to keep his tone light and informative, but he was fully aware he was staring at her. "It might be bumpy, but don't let that bother you."

"Right. No throwing up. Check." Finally, she met his gaze with a smile that was supposed to be brave, he guessed. It didn't quite make it. She looked sweet and vulnerable. That sharpness hit him again. What was wrong with him?

"Then we'll be on a regular plane when we leave Minneapolis."

"Now boarding to Minneapolis!" A man in a safety vest shouted through an open door.

"You can do this." Then, because he couldn't help himself, he gave her arm a squeeze. "I have faith in you." Color flooded her cheeks, but she didn't pull away.

"Everyone keeps telling me that." Together, they stood and began the long walk out to the tarmac. She drew in a breath.

He could feel the tension rolling off her body as they neared the small plane. One other person straggled out of the building after them. At least the flight wouldn't be crowded.

He wanted to wrap his arms around her and tell her it was all going to work out. But the guy behind them was grumbling as he barreled toward the steps, so James thought it best to get on the plane. Besides, touching her was not on his to-do list today or any other day. At least until this case was closed.

The pilot greeted them, thermos of coffee in his hands. "Morning, Mr. Carlson." He then nodded to Maggie. "Ma'am. Welcome back. We'll be up in a few. Pick any seat you want—you two and the other passenger are it this morning."

Maggie nodded, her smile a thin, tight thing on her face. "Thank you," she said, and again James marveled at how strong she sounded.

The plane had two seats on one side of the aisle, and another lonely seat on the other side. The whole thing was about fifteen rows deep. He'd been on smaller planes, but Maggie hadn't. He debated sitting separately, but only for a second. They were traveling together. Sitting together was not suggestive. He guided her to seats close to the front. Luckily, the other guy stuck to the middle of the plane, so they could have some privacy.

Privacy to do what? That was the question that James couldn't answer. They wouldn't be in the air more than forty minutes, but he knew safe time alone with Maggie was at a premium. When they were in the suite, he could barely afford to be in the same room with her. The rest of the time, they'd be at the Department of Justice, making a case for his case. Here, on this plane, he could speak with her honestly, but the other passenger and the pilot guaranteed he wouldn't cross any lines.

Maggie slid in first, staring wide-eyed out the window. She clicked the buckle over her lap and tightened it down.

Then she closed her eyes. He could see the concentration writ large across her forehead.

In a strange way, it almost hurt him to see her that nervous, to know he was making her do this. Another pang of guilt hit him midchest. He had to do something to make this better for her—but it wasn't like he could send her home. There was no going back. This case was too important. He had to put Maynard away. But this wasn't about another win, not anymore. This was about justice for Maggie. There *had* to be a way to keep her off the stand. "This is perfectly safe," was the weak thing he came up with, as if that would make it all better.

"Because you're the expert in safety, right?"

That pulled him up short. James looked over his shoulder. The other passenger was already snoring. "What?"

"I'm pretty sure I'm not pregnant, just so you know. I took several tests, just to be safe. And I've had a clean bill of health for years. You left *before* I could tell you that. Before I could ask about you."

She had him dead to rights, but his defense mechanism was hardwired. "Look, Agnes called about the case and then Nan came in and I had to get back to the office—"

She held up her hand. "I understand. The case comes first." Except she said it through clenched teeth as the door behind them shut.

Part of him wanted to feel badly about that. She was right, after all. He'd bailed the moment the call had come through. But she was also right that the case—and his career—had to come first. Ferreting out corruption was bigger than his feelings for her. He hadn't come this far to be distracted by his attraction to a woman. Not even if that woman was Maggie Eagle Heart.

Man, this was killing him. To hell with keeping his distance. He leaned in close—close enough that he could smell the warmth of her skin and the clean scent of green apples in her hair. "Maggie," he said in a voice that was loud enough that she could hear him over the engines roaring to life, "I promised to keep you safe, and that's a promise I intend to keep, on the ground and in the air."

Her eyes fluttered back open as she took a deep breath. The lines of stress eased from her forehead, and when she turned to look at him, their noses were less than six inches apart. A quick, small smile flashed over her face, and despite the ungodly hour and the nerve-racking situation, he felt a building warmth spread throughout his chest. "I have faith in you, too."

At that instant the plane began to taxi toward the runway. Maggie sucked in a hard breath and squeezed her eyes shut tight. James knew he shouldn't—couldn't—touch her, but this wasn't about sex or desire. This was about comforting another person. She had comforted him the other night—before he took it too far.

He still couldn't believe he'd crossed that line. For the last nine years, Maggie had attained an almost holy purity, abstaining from every single weakness known to man. And just because his nanny had died, James had taken the comfort Maggie had offered him and turned it sexual. Yes, the attraction between them had been there from the moment she'd walked into his office.

But James knew the truth. He was corrupting her. And now he had to take her into his world and introduce her to his people—people like Lenon, who wouldn't care about how she'd turned her life around, how she'd made something of herself. No one in D.C. would care about her as a person— no one but him.

Despite her history, Maggie was too innocent, too naive, just too damn pure. He was going to ruin her life, her reputation, and for what? Yes, he wanted justice done. But winning this case wasn't just about putting Maynard away. In D.C.,

it would be less about protecting the weak and innocent and
more—much more—about winning his case and having the
perfect record when he ran for office.

Was he really the kind of man who would do that to someone he was fond of? To *Maggie?*

He slid his hand over the one of hers that had a death grip
on the armrest. No other part of her moved, but she flipped
that hand and laced her fingers through his.

It could have been different. He could have refused to cash
in his insurance policy and let the case die. He would have
had to take his black eye and move on, but Maggie would
have been safe.

But others wouldn't, his consciousness pointed out. If he
didn't put Maynard away, the man would destroy someone
else's life. He couldn't let the case die. He had sworn to up-
hold the law. All he could do was hope that Yellow Bird came
up with something, and fast. That was the only way to protect Maggie and lock Maynard up—for good. And until that
time, Maggie was his star witness.

The plane accelerated, the force pushing them back into
their seats. James smiled. He'd always loved takeoffs and
landings, the sensation of breaking the law of gravity. He
leaned forward to look past Maggie and out the window. He
couldn't see much—it was still dark—but the lights of the
terminal were visible.

Then they were off the ground, climbing higher and higher.
The rush of flight made him feel giddy, and he was tempted
to tell Maggie to open her eyes to see the fading lights of
Pierre disappear behind them. But suddenly, the plane hit an
air pocket—a big one. The plane bumped up and then down
a few feet. Maggie let out a scream that was only muffled by
her clenched teeth.

"Folks, we're going to have a bumpy ride this morning,

so stay buckled in your seats," the pilot called back. James heard the other passenger grunt, but the snoring continued.

Damnation. As the plane hit another pocket, she clamped down on his hand so hard that she was in serious danger of breaking one or more of his fingers. "I don't want to do this anymore," she said in a whisper of panic.

Double damnation. James pried his wounded fingers away from her and slid that arm around her shoulders as he raised the armrest. Then he pulled her closer and gave her his other hand to hold. She grabbed it with both hands and held on for dear life, then burrowed her face into his chest. That weird warmth spread up the back of his neck. So he couldn't get her off this plane. He could still be the rock she clung to.

"Just a little turbulence," he said into her hair. She nodded—a tiny movement, but enough to let him know she'd heard him. He decided that if he kept talking and she kept listening, he might be able to distract her from her terror. "This flight is all takeoff and landing. There's no cruising at any altitude."

Again, the tiny nod. But this time, she shifted so that more of her body was leaning against him. It bordered on cozy.

He leaned back, enjoying the feel of her body against his. Their brief, heated coupling hadn't left time for touching. He felt the heavy weight of her breast against his chest, the silky smoothness of her hair.

All that warmth that had been doing all that building in his body went right past comforting and straight on over to desire. He prayed she wouldn't notice his sudden, inconvenient erection.

Another series of turbulent bumps saved them both. He hugged her tighter and kept on explaining what each noise and every movement meant. When they began the descent, she had calmed down enough that she was able to look out the window to see the miles of Minneapolis lights twinkling in the distance. "It's so big," she said, the wonder obvious in her voice before a huge drop sent her back into his arms.

James held her throughout the rocky landing. He'd flown a lot, but this particular landing was one of the roughest he could remember. It got to the point that he couldn't tell if he was trying to convince her or himself that each noise had a purpose. Damn it all, he'd never forgive himself for getting her killed.

Maggie let out a strangled squeak when the plane's wheels touched the runway and then the plane bounced back into the air for a brief moment. The contact took on the second attempt, and before long, they were taxiing to the terminal.

"We're down," he told her as he tried to untangle his limbs from hers.

She didn't appear to have heard him. In fact, she didn't move. Had she passed out? "Maggie?"

"Is it over?" No forced confidence this time. Instead, she sounded as if she was on the verge of sobbing.

Just then, the plane came to a stop. Moments later, the door popped open. "It's over, sweetheart," he heard himself whisper. *Sweetheart? Damn it.* "We can get off the plane now."

Maggie unbuckled the seat belt, but when she tried to stand, her knees gave out and she fell back into her seat. She made a noise that sounded like, "Orgh," as she put her head between her knees.

"You made it," he said, knowing full well his words probably weren't helping. He started to rub her back, right between her shoulder blades. "You did a great job. Now you've got to stand up and walk off this plane." He stood and more or less lifted her up. She was completely gray, and her hair was plastered to her forehead with sweat. "Come on, sweetheart. I'm right here for you."

She let him take her by the arm and guide her down the steps. They then took their time mounting the stairs that led into the terminal. By the time they got to the top, Maggie's face was now an ashy-green and her whole body was shaking. "I think I'm going to pass out," she said in a faint voice.

He looked around until he saw a smoothie stand about thirty feet away. "Come on," he said again, pulling her toward a cluster of tables in the middle of the terminal.

Once she had her head back between her knees, he hurried to get her a strawberry-banana smoothie. The smoothie worker was in no mood to hurry, and James found himself tapping his toe with impatience. "Thanks," he said in his most sarcastic tone when he finally had the smoothie in hand.

By the time he got back to where he'd left Maggie, she was sitting upright, looking slightly less green. He handed her the smoothie and waited while she downed the whole thing in under three minutes.

"You didn't eat breakfast, did you?" Her sheepish grin told him he was right. But at least she was grinning.

"I didn't want to throw up all over either of us." She couldn't look at him while she said it.

Classic mistake for a rookie flyer. "Come on. I'm buying you breakfast."

"But you already got me a smoothie."

He leveled his best don't-argue-with-me glare at her and then broke out his feral smile. She momentarily wilted before she did something unexpected. She began to laugh.

Not the response he was used to getting. He'd brought grown men—men with power and clout—to their knees with that look. And this beautiful woman was laughing at him. The odd thing was, he kind of liked it. "What?"

"Nothing," she said, her eyes still dancing.

Like hell, he thought, but she didn't say anything else. Instead, she took great care in wrapping her lips around the straw and sucking down the last of the smoothie.

Raw desire hit him hard. No, he was not going to sleep with her, but that didn't mean he wouldn't think about it.

She giggled again, and even though the airport was filling up with early-morning travelers, he had a weird feeling, as if the world was of no consequence to him and Maggie.

Before they got onto the next plane, he'd call Yellow Bird for a status report. He had to keep Maggie off the stand. If she was off the stand…well, it would make the ethical dilemma of their mutual attraction less *compromising*—for both of them. And the sooner that happened, the better it would be for everyone.

He'd never wanted a case to be over so badly in his life.

Ten

James walked down a wide space that looked more like a mall than an airport. Maggie tried not to gape like some country bumpkin, but it was almost impossible. Expensive-looking, intimidating shops sat near the more everyday newsstands. James passed them all as if he knew where he was going. All Maggie could do was try to keep up.

Finally, he stopped in front of some sort of French bakery. They got a table near the front, and James let her sit so she could watch the world walk by. A waitress brought them menus. "The omelets are really good," he said, his tone making it clear she wasn't going to get away with ordering just a bagel.

Maggie sighed in mock frustration, but secretly, she was pleased. Was it weird to enjoy someone—someone other than Nan, that was—taking care of her? It made her feel, well, *safe*. Like James had her back.

Which was something completely different than having

her front. At this forbidden thought, her cheeks warmed, so she buried her face in her menu. No way, no how could she think such things—not so soon after nearly fainting on the plane, not ever. He'd let her see his cracks once. However, a single moment of humanity didn't mean he was some sort of knight in shining armor. She knew the score. They weren't having breakfast together because this was a date. They were here because he was worried about his case. That's why he was making her go to D.C. and attend cocktail parties.

Still, she could *like* him. She'd never had a man friend before. Obviously, with that whole sex-on-a-kitchen-counter thing, she wasn't doing a great job of having one now, but she was committed to trying.

"You look better," he said after they'd ordered their food. "How are you feeling?"

Any time she wanted to stop blushing around him would be great. It would be even better if she could do that today. "I didn't think it would be that scary."

He nodded, looking thoughtful. He didn't call her stupid or silly. He *listened*. How crazy was that? "It was a rough flight, but the next one will be better." He looked her in the eyes as he leaned forward a little. It felt as if the space between them evaporated—she could almost feel him touch her. "I promise."

"You make a lot of promises." The old her wouldn't have said anything like that. But James had never known the old her. It was freeing to be able to remake herself any way she wanted. She straightened up in her chair and felt herself smile. It felt good.

Being with James felt good.

"Only the ones I intend to keep."

Did that include not sleeping with her? So much for not blushing. He watched her as the waitress brought them their food. "What?" she asked.

"I can't believe that plane ride is the scariest thing you've ever done."

She tried to shrug that off. "There's a difference between scary and stupid, you know."

He nodded in acknowledgment. "Even when you walked into that blizzard?"

Maggie was confused. He already knew all this stuff—why was he still asking about it? Then she realized he wasn't asking her about facts. He was trying to understand *why*.

Not even Rosebud had asked why. Maggie had assumed Rosebud understood. But James had assumed once, before their first meeting, and he'd promised he wouldn't do it again.

"Was I scared I was going to die?"

James nodded.

"Yeah, that was a part of it. But there was more to it than that." She tried to find the words, but how did one explain the intent to kill oneself? "I was...relieved. I was glad I was the one who was ending it. It was my choice. In this weird way, deciding to die finally gave me control of my life." James's eyes had gotten wide. "That sounds bad. I'm sorry." She didn't know why she was apologizing.

Not that her apology did anything to make James look less upset. If anything, he looked even more disturbed than he had when he'd deposed her. He pushed back from the table, looking as if he was a second away from getting up and pacing. Just as he'd looked the other night—right before he'd told her he'd have to use her testimony. She didn't like it when he looked like this. It usually meant something bad was about to happen. "What?"

"You're apologizing to me? I'm the one who should be apologizing."

"The plane ride wasn't that bad," she lied, feeling lame as the words left her mouth. He was making her nervous.

He leveled those beautiful eyes at her. "I didn't give you

time to choose. The other night. I had no business making that choice for you."

Was he apologizing for...what? For having sex with her? For *wanting* to have sex with her? For so quickly turning their relationship from professional to personal? Just thinking about the interlude on the counter made Maggie's insides go warm and gooey. What was she supposed to say? "In case you didn't notice, you didn't force me to do anything I didn't want to do."

"That's irrelevant."

"Like hell it is." Sex was many things, but "irrelevant" wasn't one of them. She leaned forward, tapping a finger on the table to emphasize her point as she dropped her voice. "You said you wanted me. Did it ever occur to you that I wanted you, too?" He opened his mouth to protest, but she cut him off. "And it's not irrelevant. I'm an adult, fully capable of consenting or not consenting of my own free will."

A strange mix of emotions washed over his face. "I should have been more careful, though."

The conversation needed to move away from the whole sex thing—the sooner, the better. Talking about it was thinking about it, and she couldn't afford to keep thinking about it. "When does our plane leave? For D.C.?"

He held her gaze for a moment longer. Maggie was afraid they weren't going to be moving away from the sex thing—or that they would be moving someplace even more unnerving. But the second passed, and James agreed to her unspoken choice. "We depart at 10:10. We've got another three hours."

A gentle smile changed everything tense or worried about him, and suddenly she was sitting across from the most handsome man she'd ever seen. Warmth—different from the heat that made her blush—pooled low in her belly. So much for moving away from that sex thing.

"We should make sure we eat some food before we board. There's lots to do here—shopping, people watching."

"There's not much in Aberdeen," she said, feeling a little shy. Not that there was anything wrong with Walmart or JCPenney, but she hated admitting how little she knew about his world. Everything she knew about shopping came from a *Real Housewives of* wherever show—and those people weren't *real*. Not like James. She wouldn't fit in his world, that much was blindingly obvious, and to try was delusional at best and suicidal at worst. But she could enjoy this time with him. The clock was ticking, but she wouldn't take this interlude for granted. "This won't be bad—for the case, right? If we wander around?"

"I know Yellow Bird will turn up something else. As long as…" Maggie nodded, hoping he wouldn't say it out loud. "As long as we keep this professional, we can wander around, see what catches our eye." He almost—but not quite—winked at her. "We've got to see the Snoopy statue, too. Nan will get a kick out of that picture. We'll be in D.C. until four tomorrow afternoon—is there anything you want to see? D.C. is a wonderful place. I'd like to show you around. We could hit a museum or the Lincoln Memorial…" His voice trailed off as he whipped out his phone and began scrolling. "The Museum of the American Indian? I don't think we can do the White House—too late to get on the list…"

We. Maggie sat in wonder at this man while he reviewed the entire list of tourist attractions in D.C. He was doing his level best to make sure that she had *fun*. Her tummy comfortably full, a cup of fancy coffee in her hand, sitting in an airport across from one of the nicest, smartest and—honestly, now—*hottest* men she'd ever talked to. She had a weird, out-of-body, out-of-life feeling. This was someone else's life—Rosebud's maybe, but not hers.

James glanced up at her and smiled. Not a quiet or gentle

thing, but the full-force, happy-to-see-you, great-teeth *smile*. Not because he wanted something from her. Because he *was* happy to see her, to be *here* with her.

She knew she shouldn't let that raw joy get to her. She should be putting up a little wall around her heart——a thick, sturdy wall to keep the thousand small kindnesses he showed her from making her fall for him. She shouldn't appreciate his making sure she had a good breakfast. She shouldn't admire his understanding about the turbulent plane ride. She shouldn't enjoy his planning something fun for them to do together. She shouldn't find him so *damn* attractive.

But she did.

And she had fallen for him.

They spent two hours wandering around the airport mall. JCPenney it wasn't. James insisted on taking her picture with a statue of Snoopy that was twice as big as she was. Maggie bought Nan a T-shirt with a Minnesota moose on it. They bought cookies and drank sodas and snickered at the outfits people chose to wear in public. It would have felt like a date, if she were still in junior high.

The not-date went well until they entered an expensive-looking jewelry store. "Rosebud probably mentioned that Lenon has these mandatory cocktail parties. He'll expect you to go so he can judge how you handle a hostile environment. It would be best if you looked the part," James said by way of apology.

"Rosebud gave me a dress, just in case." James nodded in approval and they began to look around.

Maggie decided to splurge on a pair of fake diamond stud earrings to go with her black cocktail dress. James agreed the pear-cut ones looked best, and they were on clearance for forty-five dollars.

"We have a coordinating pendant," the saleslady said in

her smooth-as-pudding voice as she removed a necklace from the case. She casually flipped the price tag to the front—a hundred and twenty-five dollars was too rich for Maggie's blood. But before she could politely decline, the saleslady went on. "Or, we have this stunning luxury tennis necklace."

Maggie's eyes tried hard to pop out of their sockets as the saleslady unlocked a separate case and pulled out a necklace that looked as if it was made of solid diamonds. "This is regularly 3,890 dollars, but we're having a special on it this week."

"*How* much?" Maggie's voice came out as a strangled whisper. Maybe her ears had stopped working, but it sounded like the woman had said *thousand,* when *hundred* was beyond her means.

"Two thousand five hundred," the saleslady replied, like any of this made sense. "It's twenty-seven carats, total weight."

That clarification didn't improve Maggie's thunderstruck feeling. She leaned over to look at the name of the store. Still Erwin Pearl—not Tiffany or anything. Then she stretched to see the case where the necklace had come from: Affordable Luxury in Cubic Zirconia. Was this woman serious—two thousand five hundred dollars for *fake* diamonds? On *sale?*

Speechless, Maggie turned to James and was shocked to find him reaching for the necklace. "Try it on," he said, undoing the clasp and waiting for her to turn around.

"Are you kidding?" She didn't even want to touch the thing, for fear she might break it and be out two thousand five hundred.

"Do I look like I'm kidding?" Instead of waiting for an answer, he stepped around her and lowered the necklace until its cool weight rested against her skin. It was heavy, the sort of necklace that demanded awareness of its sheer extravagance.

"Stunning," the saleslady said in the kind of voice that

all salespeople used when they had suckers on the line, and James had the nerve to nod in agreement.

"I can't afford this," Maggie whispered to James. "I can't afford the cheap one. I can barely afford the earrings." Shame rushed through her. This was all wrong. She wasn't the kind of person who belonged at airports, jetting off to the capital of the whole country to take a meeting with the most powerful lawyer in the land. She didn't belong here, with James—not now, not *ever*.

When she raised her eyes, she was shocked to see a hardness in his gaze that made him look cold and calculating. She'd only seen him look like that once before—the first time she'd met him, when he'd tried to bluff her with intimidation. With exact precision, his eyes flicked over her—her hair, her face, her ears with the yet-to-be-purchased earrings still in them and the necklace that felt like a lead weight around her neck. He was sizing her up. And Maggie knew she would come up wanting. When it came to James Carlson's world, she would always come up wanting.

The salesclerk cleared her throat. "Of course, the earrings that were designed to complement that necklace are also on sale." She pulled a dangly set with huge, pear-shaped, not-real diamonds out of the case. "Both the necklace and the earrings would be thirty-one hundred dollars."

Three *grand* for fake diamonds. Her Jeep wasn't worth that much, and she used that on a regular basis. James picked up the earrings and held them against Maggie's head. Instead of the normal heat she felt from him, his hands felt as if he'd just pulled them out of a freezer.

"Your dress is black?"

What did that have to do with anything? She wasn't getting this jewelry. At this rate, she'd be lucky if she didn't pass out from sticker shock in the middle of the store.

James handed the saleslady the earrings, then motioned

for Maggie to turn around. His fingers traced along her nape, then the weight of the necklace was gone. She fumbled the cheap earrings out of her ears, wondering how on earth she could buy them now without looking like a jerk.

"Well?" The saleslady's hope made her sound expectant.

James looked at Maggie, then at the jewelry, then at Maggie again. She would never measure up to whatever standard he was holding her against. She would never be the woman he wanted, the woman he needed, and the sooner they all realized it, the better off they'd be.

But she couldn't open her mouth to tell him that. She couldn't just tell him she wasn't worth the time and effort. She had some pride. Hell, after this little soul-crushing lesson in rich versus poor, it was blindingly clear that her pride was the only thing she could still afford.

James pulled a credit card out of his wallet. "I'll take them."

Suddenly, Maggie moved. She grabbed James's arm and yanked him back from the counter. "What are you doing?"

Now, finally, his face softened. "You're going into my world, Maggie. You've got to look the part. I have *some* money," he added, cutting off her first line of defense. "There's a chance that you'll meet people—my people— and they'll judge you in the blink of an eye. We have to be ready for any contingency."

So she went with the second line of defense. "Isn't buying jewelry 'compromising' a witness?"

"It's a business expense. I've bought other witnesses clothes for trial before."

"I won't accept it." Yep. Still had her pride. That gave her a strangely comforting feeling deep in her belly. She could not be bought. Not even for three grand.

James's smile was the most dangerous mix of tender and

sweet she'd ever seen. "Yes," he said, his voice low as he ran a hand down her arm—a gesture of possession, not of comfort. "You will."

Eleven

Maggie was silent. She didn't say anything when the clerk handed them the gift-wrapped boxes in a bag. She didn't speak when he took her into a wireless store and bought her the latest smartphone. She didn't protest, complain about the cost or even thank him when he had the clerk connect it to her email and load up some games she could play.

She said nothing.

This stony silence continued while she dutifully ate the General Tso's chicken he ordered her. She didn't so much as squeak when the door of the plane *whumped* shut, or when the plane took off. She sat in her seat, eyes closed, hands lightly gripping the armrests.

James was befuddled. He could have sworn women liked to get presents, especially jewelry. Yeah, impulsively dropping thirty-one hundred was a lot. He knew that. But he also knew that dime-store fakes wouldn't pass muster in D.C. Same thing with the phone. Even legal assistants from South Dakota needed cell phones. She *had* to look the part. He couldn't risk alerting anyone outside the case that she was a key witness. He was still banking on Yellow Bird finding something that would keep Maggie off the stand. And he couldn't let anyone in the DOJ know what she really was to him.

A part of him was pissed off, and he wasn't sure why. If Yellow Bird didn't come through, then James was going to ruin Maggie's hard-won reputation by putting her on the stand. He was personally going to destroy the life she'd worked so hard to make for herself. If he were his father, it would be all in a day's work. People got hurt. People got used.

But James wasn't his father. He had personal and professional codes. And he'd broken the most important one by getting involved with Maggie. If anyone found out about him and Maggie, he could kiss this case goodbye. He could kiss the White House goodbye. He'd known that well in advance, but in his moment of weakness, it hadn't been enough to stop him. It was almost as if he'd wanted to screw up his future electability.

But worse was knowing that, if he put her on the stand, Maggie's name would be out there. And if he had to do that, the responsibility would rest entirely on his shoulders. It was bad enough that Agnes had already handed Maggie's file over to the defense as a part of discovery.

James knew he was the one who hadn't double-checked the wiretaps. He hadn't played by the rules. He'd put her at risk. The least he could do was buy her something pretty to make up for it.

He'd always thought he was a smart guy, but for the life of him, he couldn't figure out where he stood with her. So he left her alone while he stewed in his own thoughts.

Not that that helped. If he was looking for clarity, he wasn't going to find it. He'd gotten…involved, one could say, with a witness. It would have been bad enough just to have slept with her, but to have all these *feelings?* To want her? To worry about her? To have that urge to protect her, no matter what? He was hard-pressed to remember a time he'd felt this way about any woman, much less a witness. And that was the problem, in a nutshell. He had to get things back under control, and fast.

At one point, she jumped a little. He looked over to see a look of gentle peace on her face. The innocence of her beauty hit him midgut. She'd disappeared into the ladies' room before boarding and come back out with her makeup on and her hair twisted up. Now, though, her lips were slightly parted, her head propped up against the window. A few pieces of hair had come loose, framing her face with softness.

That urge to make it up to her—he was going to have to keep that in check. What she needed, he realized, wasn't payback. It was protection. Expensive necklaces and gadgets weren't enough. He'd promised to protect her—and that meant not only from her past, but from his present.

The captain came over the intercom and announced that they would be arriving at the terminal in Dulles in forty-five minutes.

With a shudder, she shook herself awake, meeting his gaze with a hesitant smile. "Hi."

She made him ache in ways that had nothing to do with his body and everything to do with his heart. "Hey. We'll be landing soon. How are you doing?"

She stretched out, taking full advantage of the first-class seats. "I fell asleep."

James grinned at the wonder in her voice. "That you did." He again fought the urge to touch her. "This flight was much smoother."

She gave him another tiny smile before she appeared to remember that she was mad at him. James didn't give her the chance to retreat this time. "Listen, I didn't mean to over-whelm you earlier."

She froze, but quickly regained her composure. "It's fine. Really."

"You don't have to keep any of those things. We can return the necklace when we go back through Minneapolis tomorrow."

Pink flushed across her cheeks. "It seemed like a lot of money for fake stuff, you know? And I don't have anyone to call, really." She shot him a sideways glance. "Just you and Rosebud."

He wanted to tell her that the money was worth it, because that particular fake was indistinguishable from the real, and that's what he needed her to be on this trip. But he didn't. Instead, he nodded as the plane dipped toward Dulles.

By the time the wheels bounced down, Maggie had undergone a minitransformation. She'd smoothed her hair back. She'd squared her shoulders, straightened her spine and put on this air of superiority that even impressed him. Her polished demeanor didn't falter when they got off the plane and found they had someone waiting for them.

"Mr. Carlson, how good to see you again." The uniformed limo driver was standing in a crowd with other drivers, but James would have recognized the tall black man with graying temples anywhere.

James met him with a hearty handshake. "Desmond, we weren't expecting you."

Damn it, his mother knew he was in town. Why else would she have sent Desmond? At least this would be a good test of Maggie's professional persona.

"Desmond, this is Maggie Eagle Heart, legal assistant to Rosebud Armstrong. She's assisting me with a case. Ms. Eagle Heart, this is Desmond Pyatt, my parents' driver."

Desmond nodded deferentially. "Let me get those bags for you, ma'am."

Maggie stood stock-still. James could almost see her trying to guess the correct response. "Thank you, Desmond. It's a pleasure to make your acquaintance."

Satisfied with this, Desmond took her and James's cases and led the way to the car. Ah, James thought when they stepped out into the D.C. swelter, Mother had sent the Bentley. Wonderful. She was in a take-over-the-world mood.

Maggie hesitated before climbing into the backseat while Desmond held the door for her. James slid in after her and promptly sat on a thick envelope—the kind used for formal invitations. He glanced at Maggie, who was staring in shock at the custom leather interior, the built-in cocktail cabinet and the surround-sound speakers. Then she blew out a long breath and gave James the kind of look that said, *Are you serious?*

"This is my mother's preferred car," he explained as he opened the envelope.

"Darling James," the note began.

I'm so glad you've decided to come home for a visit. I've had your rooms prepared and I'm looking forward to chatting with you about your plans for the future. Todd is hosting a cocktail party tonight, which begins at nine. Please be prompt, as Pauline will be awaiting your arrival with great interest.

Regards,
Julia

Double damn.

"Desmond," James said, lowering the window between them, "please take us to the Watergate."

"Mrs. Carlson has your suite ready at the house, sir."

Maggie's eyes got wider. He'd tried to warn her about this. Apparently, he hadn't done a good job. At least they were safe from prying eyes here in the car.

"I'm not here for a visit, Desmond, a fact my mother is fully aware of. Take us to the Watergate. And knock off that *sir* crap. She's not here now."

Maggie shot him a wild look.

"It's okay," he reassured her. "Desmond's been driving me around for—how many years, now, Desmond?"

"Going on twenty. Been driving you around since you were *Jamie*." There was no mistaking the gentle teasing in the older man's voice.

"Jamie?" Maggie's voice was pitched low, so that only James could hear her. "Really?"

He grinned at her. "That was a long time ago."

"Took him to all those dances—remember your first homecoming? Boy," Desmond said, and James heard the sadness creep in. "Remember Stephanie? We sure lost a good one in her."

Of course he remembered Stephanie. "Hard to believe it's been almost seven years."

"Old girlfriend?" Maggie had relaxed a little bit now, but he could see that she still wasn't completely comfortable.

James debated not saying anything, because he knew this information was not going to go over well. But Maggie was going to be at a cocktail party with his mother and her chosen daughter-in-law. Odds were good that someone would bring up Stephanie. Knowledge might not be power in this particular situation, but it was a hell of a lot better than a straight-up ambush.

"Stephanie was more a 'friend who was a girl' than a 'girlfriend.' We went to a lot of dances together—the safety date." Maggie nodded in understanding, but James had to wonder how many school dances she'd made it to. Not many, if any at all. Well, tonight she'd get a taste of what she'd been missing.

"What happened to her?"

"She died in a car accident." Maybe Maggie already knew. Maybe this wouldn't be so bad. "She was married to someone you know." He gave her a look that he hoped reminded her she was supposed to be a legal assistant. "Thomas Yellow Bird?"

She choked, her hand flying to her mouth. But she got herself under control and managed a faint "Oh?"

For a man who prided himself on a thorough preparation of his witnesses for any situation, he was doing a lousy job. The analytical side of his brain wondered if the befuddling effect Maggie had on him was to blame.

"Those were some good days, huh?" Desmond hadn't picked up on Maggie's shock. "Hasn't been the same since you hightailed it out of D.C."

This was familiar territory for James. Desmond appreciated his job and all the benefits that went with it, but they both knew that working for Julia Carlson could be *challenging,* to say nothing of his father. The car had always been a safe spot for both Desmond and James to blow off steam.

"You should come out west, Desmond. Might do you good to see life outside of the Beltway." As he said it, though, he watched Maggie. She still held her hand to her mouth, and the color was draining from her face.

He and Desmond talked some more, but James wasn't paying attention to the conversation. He was focused on the woman next to him. She'd ducked her head forward, so that it was almost between her knees. She was breathing heavily. He had to do something fast, or she was going to black out on him. He opened the cocktail cabinet and rummaged around until he found a can of La Croix seltzer water. It was the only nonalcoholic beverage he had.

"Drink this." He held the fizzing can near her face. She

weakly shook her head *no,* but he repeated, "*Drink* this, Maggie."

Hell. This level of "overwhelmed" made the silent treatment look like a sunny day at the beach. But she took the can and drank it.

This was never going to work. Maggie wouldn't be able to pull off the level of artifice D.C.—and his family—required. She was too honest, too innocent. Instead, he was going to drag her further down into his mud and if Yellow Bird didn't come up with something else to use against Maynard, James would end up obliterating everything she'd made for herself.

By the time they got to the Watergate, Maggie was sitting up again. She took Desmond's proffered hand when she got out of the car, and walked with slow precision into the massive lobby.

"She okay?" Desmond asked as he unloaded the bags.

"First-time flyer," James replied, hoping that would be enough.

"I hear that." James fished out a fifty and tried to hand it to Desmond. "Not gonna happen, and you know it."

"Mother's going to tear you a new one for bringing us here, Desmond. The least I can do is make it up to you." Desmond gave him a long look before James tucked the bill back into his pocket. "Are we going to see you again?"

"I gotta drive your parents tonight, but I can take you back to the airport tomorrow. When's your flight?"

James watched Maggie disappear through the doors. She looked as if she knew where she was going, but he couldn't let her wander too far. "We might want to do some sightseeing tomorrow. Can I call you in the morning?"

Suspicion wafted across Desmond's face, but he was too experienced in how D.C. worked to give anything away. "Sure can. Good seeing you again, James."

"You, too, Desmond." The two men shook hands, and then James went to find Maggie.

He hoped she was waiting for him.

Twelve

The key to surviving was not to talk. This was what Maggie had decided. Far better to let James do the talking with the front-desk people, all of whom were wearing fancy matching outfits and speaking in serious voices. And with the bell-boy, who loaded up their bags. She didn't know what to say, anyway.

Tommy had been married to James's best friend. And she had died in a car accident. Maggie wasn't sure why this information was throwing her for such a loop, but it was. If the world around her was a web of connections, she felt like a stuck fly, waiting to be some spider's dinner.

And that car? *With* a driver?

What the hell had she gotten herself into?

The situation did not improve when the bellboy showed them into their room. Their *apartment* was more like it—the place was huge, with one whole wall that was nothing but glass. Leather sofas, nice tables—even the lamps were classy.

The whole thing was twice the size of the little dugout house she shared with Nan. James took a tour of the place, but Maggie couldn't move. She couldn't even think.

James tipped the bellboy, and mercifully, the man left. Immediately, James came over and put his hands on her shoulders. "Are you okay?"

If she were really some legal assistant, she could probably come up with a witty, intelligent-sounding response that would make both of them laugh in that polite, not-really-funny sort of way. Everyone here probably did that. No one here felt as if they were drowning while they walked around.

"Breathe, Maggie." James's hands moved from her shoulders to her back, and suddenly he had pulled her into his chest. His scent—woodsy and clean—surrounded her as she struggled to get her mind working properly. "It's okay. You're doing a great job, sweetheart."

"It's not okay." As much as she wanted to stay in his arms, she couldn't. She pushed him away. The action freed her, and suddenly she was pacing in wide circles—because there was enough room in this place to do that. "It's *not* okay. Tommy was married to your best friend?"

"For about three years."

Maggie knew she was going faster and faster, but she couldn't stop. She'd always poured her nervous energy into her beadwork, baking, gardening—something that let her work through it. Here? She had nothing but her feet. "Were you and Tommy friends? Before you were a team?"

"Yes."

She would give James this—he was one cool cucumber over there. Part of her wanted to calm the hell down and be cool with him. The other part of her got angrier. Why hadn't she known any of this? Did Tommy—did James—think she was too stupid to handle the truth?

"But he changed after Stephanie died," James added. "I don't think we're friends so much anymore. Just a team."

The way he said it—she couldn't stop to figure out which friend he was sadder about losing—Stephanie or Tommy. "What about Rosebud?"

The question hung in the air. James looked miserable. She shouldn't have asked that—she shouldn't be jealous of whatever James and Rosebud had been. But she had to know—was James a love-them-and-leave-them man?

He half sat, half collapsed onto a couch—one of four in the room. "She thought I wouldn't come to South Dakota—that I couldn't handle the rez or the way people lived out there. She thought I wanted what my parents wanted—and, back then, I did." He looked up her. "But now…I don't know what I want anymore."

Sweet Lord in heaven, he was serious. He was looking at her and talking about a future that didn't involve D.C. or the Oval Office.

"What about me? What are we, James?"

He pushed himself off the couch and walked toward her. With more tenderness than she had ever felt, he brushed a strand of hair away from her face, then cupped her cheek in his hand. With deliberation, he lowered his lips to hers—a simple kiss.

But one that changed everything, nonetheless.

"I know what we should be, and what we shouldn't be," James whispered as he touched his forehead to hers. "But we aren't either one. We're something else, and I don't know what to do about it."

They stood there, arms wrapped around each other, for what seemed like both a very short and a very long time. Maybe it was peace, maybe it was acceptance of a situation beyond her control—but whatever it was, Maggie felt the tension leave her body. It was strangely comforting that he wasn't a hundred percent confident about this fine mess they'd gotten themselves into. Maggie felt less lost, knowing that.

His phone rang, shattering the protective quiet that had surrounded them.

"Damn," James muttered, more to himself than to her. He glanced at a huge, artsy clock hanging on the wall. "We need to leave in fifteen minutes."

Something else would have to wait.

But for how long?

Dressed in her white interview suit and matching shoes, Maggie kept her chin up and her mouth shut as they entered the Department of Justice. This office had to have the same number of people scurrying around it as lived in the whole of Aberdeen, she concluded, which was disorienting enough. But Maggie also felt out of place. In South Dakota, she'd blended in. An Indian woman driving a beat-up Jeep was a part of the everyday landscape—something she'd used to go completely unnoticed for years. James had been the one to stand out back there. Not too many people wore the expensive suits he liked, or talked with the same inflection.

Now? The situation was completely reversed. Maggie could feel hundreds—if not thousands—of eyes on her. Judging her. Deciding if she was one of "them" or not. In that instant, she understood the expensive fake jewelry and the phone—and they weren't even at the cocktail party yet. She'd completely underestimated the size of the magnifying glass she was operating under.

James, on the other hand, was all but invisible here. The place was crawling with serious men and women wearing a sea of gray, blue and tan suits, each one more tailored than the last. The Office of the Attorney General of the United States made their hotel room look like a hovel. Marble floors, oil paintings on the wall and furniture that was so large and polished it should have been in a museum. Behind a so-organized-it-hurt desk sat a middle-aged woman in a pale pink suit.

"Laura," James said with a polite nod.

Laura shot him a scolding look. "You're late, James."

"How late?" Maggie might be hearing things, but she thought she heard him smile through his words.

"So late you're almost on time." No, Maggie hadn't been imagining things. Both James and the receptionist were telling the same joke. What had Rosebud said? Lenon was always an hour behind schedule? "He's on a conference call right now, but—" she glanced at her computer "—he should be off in a few minutes. Have a seat and I'll have Jeannette get you some coffee."

Maggie watched in amazement as the receptionist made a call. Apparently, this place had a pecking order so detailed that even the receptionists had receptionists.

While they sat, James got out his phone and, giving her one of the looks he used to tell her to play along, began sending text messages. Right. She had a phone—time to whip that bad boy out.

Head bent, she watched what James did out of the corner of her eyes. She wished she hadn't been in such a twit before, because then he could have shown her how to use it. But he seemed to understand her dilemma, taking it one step at a time while she copied his movements. Before she knew it, she was reading her email. Wild.

You know, she thought to herself, *this isn't so bad.* Email from anywhere, receptionists' receptionists bringing her coffee, a big hotel room, a family driver. A girl could get used to this.

Which was ridiculous—she should not be getting used to anything. This was not her world; James was not her man.

Hell, these clothes weren't even hers. It was all just one giant lie.

Not too much time had passed before Laura informed James that the attorney general would see him. "Don't forget to breathe," James whispered to her as he headed back through the huge double doors.

"You, too," she whispered back, trying to keep her attention on her phone and not the man walking away from her. The doors shut behind him, leaving her the only person in the waiting room.

She busied herself by pecking out an email to Nan about the crazy plane trip and the new phone and the car ride. She left out the parts where she flipped out or almost passed out—no need to worry Nan. She kept hitting the wrong buttons and weird words popped up where she least expected them. Finally, she gave up and sent the message, hoping Nan would understand that Maggie didn't "louver" her.

She was trying to figure out how to play a game where the birds were angry, when the shouting interrupted her concentration. The volume of words that suddenly poured out from behind those closed doors was unnerving at best, terrifying at worst. She couldn't understand what, exactly, was being said, but she could guess. The attorney general wasn't happy about something, and sooner or later, that something would come back around to her.

That old feeling of having done something wrong took root in her belly. It was all well and good to say she wasn't going to shy away from standing up to Tommy, or even James. Deep down, she knew both men cared about her—in their own *fond* ways. Todd Lenon, however, didn't give a rat's ass for her, and that scared her. A lot.

"Ms. Eagle Heart?" Maggie snapped her head up to see Laura the receptionist waiting on her. "Mr. Lenon will see you now."

Was she nervous right now? Oh, yes. Only a fool would be a-okay with this lousy setup. But was she going to hide and whimper and beg for mercy? Hell, *no*.

She slid her phone back into her bag and took her time getting to her feet. The ivory heels Rosebud had picked out for her were starting to seriously pinch her toes, but now was not the time to stumble around. Laura waited patiently when Maggie stopped to take a couple of deep breaths before going through the open door. James had faith in her. For his sake, she had to prove that his faith wasn't misplaced. She didn't want to disappoint him.

James was sitting at a marble-topped table, pouting in the most professional way possible. Not a good sign.

Mr. Lenon had his back to her. He was standing at a bar, pouring a rich color into a glass that caught the light from the windows and threw a rainbow prism around the room. His pants were close-cut, and he had on a vest. When the door shut behind her, Maggie stopped and waited.

"Carlson tells me you're our star witness now," Mr. Lenon began with no other introductions.

How the heck was she supposed to respond to that? She glanced at James, who shrugged. *I could use a little more help here,* she thought. "It seems that's the case."

Mr. Lenon turned around, leaning back against the bar, swirling his drink in his hand. "Indeed." He took his time looking her up and down, and Maggie suddenly realized she had to sell herself to this man—not her body, but the whole concept of her existence. She had to sell him on the fact that she was an upstanding citizen worthy enough to build a case on.

Faking it, she thought. *That's what he wants.* So she plastered on a coy smile and did a slow pirouette.

Mr. Lenon cocked an eyebrow at her. "Give me one reason why I should put a hooker on the stand."

The flash of anger felt good. It felt powerful. She wasn't here to be kicked around. "I can give you several. First off, it's *former* hooker. I'm a successful businesswoman in good standing in the Aberdeen community, as well as the larger internet community of American Indian dancers. Second, my record has been clean for nearly ten years. In that time, I completed my GED as well as twenty-four hours of college courses. Third, it's the right thing to do. You're taking a stand for the forgotten people you've sworn to protect. Even if we're poor, even if we've done things we're not proud of, we still deserve the same legal protection as the rich and powerful." Lenon snorted into his drink. Not good enough. So she kept going. "But those aren't the real reasons."

The corner of Lenon's mouth curled up. It might have been a smile, but it looked more like a sneer. "No?"

Oh, he was a pompous, arrogant ass, and his condescending attitude pissed her off. "The real reason you'll put a *former* hooker on the stand is that it makes you look good. Standing up for the little guy, cleaning up corruption—especially corruption that may have taken place under your watch? That's the sort of thing that plays awfully well in a future campaign." James had said as much over dinner. It was easy for crusaders to get elected, and Todd Lenon didn't look like the kind of man who was done climbing his ladder. Maggie just hoped she wasn't too far off the mark. "*That's* why you'll put me on the stand."

As her anger faded, she realized she'd accused the attorney general of fostering corruption. *Oops.* She hadn't meant to, but when she'd opened her mouth, the words had flowed as if they had a life all their own. Maggie looked at James to see how badly she'd overstepped her boundaries and was surprised to see a smile on his face.

"I told you," James said to Lenon without taking his eyes off her. "She's a credible witness." Maggie warmed at the compliment. She hadn't let him down. She hadn't let her-self down.

All those good feelings were short-lived. Lenon tossed back his drink. Unless he did something jerky again, and soon, Maggie was in serious danger of losing the power of her anger and wilting under the weight of her nerves.

Finally, he set his empty glass down, crossed his arms and did everything but sit in judgment of her. *Faking it,* she thought, squaring her shoulders and remembering to breathe.

"This is your last chance, Carlson. One more setback, and I'm pulling you off the case and dropping all charges. You *will* take the fall, and that's the sort of thing that does not play well on the campaign trail. Do I make myself clear?"

"Absolutely," James said, swinging to his feet. "Thank you for your time, sir."

Lenon waved him away as he turned back toward the bar. Really? Maggie thought. How much did the man drink?

James motioned her toward the door, but they didn't get far. "Oh, James—we're having a little get-together tonight at the club. You'll stop by, won't you?"

"I have every intention of being there."

"Ms. Eagle Heart," Lenon added as they were almost out the door, "you'll be joining us, won't you?"

She *so* did not want to spend any more time with this man or with people he considered friends. But in for a penny, in for a pound. "Of course, Mr. Lenon."

Thirteen

James was trying not to pace, but Maggie had been in her bedroom for close to three hours. She'd been exhausted when they got back from the meeting, so James had ordered some dinner from room service. Then he'd told her to take a nap, that he'd wake her up when she needed to get ready. Which he had done. Almost an hour ago.

What had been hard about that was just knocking on the door—not going in, not stretching out on the bed next to her, not kissing her awake. His restraint gave him a dull, hangover-type headache. Perfect preparation for a cocktail party with his parents in attendance, really.

It hadn't taken a legal genius to see that an exhausted woman braving the viper pit of Beltway socializing was a recipe for disaster. He'd taken advantage of the extra time to call Rosebud and Agnes and let them know what had happened with Lenon.

Plus, he'd needed to get his own thoughts in order. For a

lawyer who was always prepared, he felt as if he was dropping every ball when it came to Maggie. He was supposed to be protecting her—but she was the one who'd walked into Lenon's office as though she owned it. She was the one who had protected his sorry backside—not the other way around. He'd thought she couldn't do it—then she did it and more.

Maggie was something real. Her honesty gave her a strength that he wasn't sure he could match. It seemed a twisted fact of fate that someone as resourceful, resilient and capable as Maggie would be automatically disqualified from serving the public just because she'd survived a horrible childhood. What did it say about his world that people like his parents would toss out someone like Maggie for not being born rich and privileged?

James was used to people expecting the world—literally—from him. Maggie didn't expect that from him. She just expected him to be a decent human being, and he found himself wanting to meet her expectations. Why did that feel as if it was inconsistent with his presidential goals? Being around her made James feel vulnerable. He liked her—too much. His feelings for her were a huge liability. He didn't like having liabilities.

"Maggie?" he called out through the shut door. He wasn't going in, not after Lenon's not-so-idle threat to make sure he'd never do anything but chase ambulances for the rest of his life if he blew this case. Tampering with a witness fell squarely into the middle of "blowing it." At least he'd talked to Yellow Bird while Maggie had rested. Yellow Bird thought he had something in Omaha. "We need to get going."

"Okay." At least she sounded perkier. A few seconds later, the door opened. "I need a little help. I'm not good at these zippers."

And just like that, James found himself staring at Maggie's back. Her bare back. The dress—a nice little black number—hung open, revealing a wide swath of bare skin and the thin band of a black bra. He could see the edges of her tattoo peeking out from under the dress, which gave her an air of sophisticated danger. Her hair had been freed from the restrictive twist, and now hung in loose waves draped over the front of her dress.

His blood pounding, James went hard in an instant. Because their first time had been so fierce and uncontrolled, he hadn't had the chance to stop and appreciate the woman's body—which was a crying shame, because she had a *hell* of a body. All he wanted to do was run his hands down that bare skin and peel the dress away.

Thank God Maggie couldn't see his sudden discomfort. Instead, she stood, patiently waiting for him to act like a gentleman. She trusted him. He better start acting like a man worthy of it.

Breathing in through his nose and out through his mouth, he grasped the zipper and began to tug it up. With each click, that much of her skin disappeared from view—and touch. James scrambled to think of something—anything—that would distract him. William Howard Taft never really wanted to be president. He wanted to be chief justice of the Supreme Court. Only guy to be both. Taft was a big man. He'd been an ambassador to the Philippines. Went to Yale.

This recitation of facts helped—until James got the zipper just above the bra strap. Suddenly, the zipper wouldn't close—did this dress even fit? "Um…"

"We got it zipped in Rosebud's office," Maggie said. Her voice was small, and maybe a little irritated. Was she as turned on as he was? "One second."

Then she leaned forward and moved her hands toward her midsection. He felt her body shift against the dress, and then the zipper continued on its way up.

It was only after he'd taken a vital step away from her that he realized what she'd been doing—lifting up each breast so the dress could fit around them. A fact confirmed when she turned around and, while still looking down the most luscious chest he'd ever had the pleasure of witnessing in person, said, "See? I knew it would zip! We had to go with this one because it was the only one that hid the tattoo. Do these shoes look okay?"

"Yeah," he said, not looking at her feet. "You look great." *Something else.* That's what this was. That's what *she* was.

Head still down—thank God she wasn't looking at him—she walked back to the table and picked up the necklace. "Please," she said in a sweet voice as she turned around, lifted her hair away from her neck and handed the necklace back over her shoulder. "And thank you."

The conflict of interest was going to kill him, because he was interested—and that was the conflict. He placed the necklace around her throat and, hands shaking, managed to get it latched. He was afraid to move. Hell, even breathing wasn't that safe—her clean scent, baby powder and hotel lotion—

The next thing he knew, he'd leaned forward and pressed his lips against the side of her neck. Her warm skin shivered under his touch, but she didn't pull away.

He. Should. Not.

She expected better of him, and he wanted to be better for her.

But he wasn't as strong as she was. Maybe he would never be, and fighting it was pointless. He wrapped his arms around her waist and pulled her back into his chest, thereby rendering the point of whether or not she could *see* his awkward state moot, because she sure as hell was going to *feel* it.

Let her. He wanted her to know how much she messed him up—him, of all people. He'd always been the guy who followed the rules. He was a man of the law. He'd taken an oath—an oath he'd spent his life upholding. He knew who he was, and who he was *supposed* to be.

She sighed, her body molding itself to his as she reached back and ran her fingers through his hair—pulling his head more into her neck.

Yes, he knew who he was supposed to be, all right. And that was the problem. Because, whenever he was around her, he couldn't remember who that man was.

Before he could feel one of those luscious breasts first-hand, though, she pulled away and took three long steps to the other side of the room. She stood there, head down and arms at her side. That conflicted interest ripped through him again—he knew he shouldn't do *anything,* but he wanted to follow her into the room with the nice big bed, and forget all about that stupid cocktail party.

"James…" Her voice quivered, as if maybe she was…what? Trying not to cry? Desperate for his touch again?

Want me, James thought. *Want me as much as I want you.* But she didn't.

"Don't do that again."

She was right, of course. Completely, totally, a hundred percent correct. It still hit him like a punch to the kidneys.

Maybe she took his silence as pouting or something, because she spun around and stared at him. For a moment, she looked—hell, he didn't know. Flattered? Embarrassed? Whatever it was, her cheeks were tinted a warm pink, and she pursed her lips into a completely kissable pout. James realized he was physically shaking from the effort of restraining himself.

Which was the correct thing to do, because the moment of kissability passed and Maggie's shyness turned mean. "You can't look at me like that."

James struggled to clear his throat. "Like what?"

"Look," she said, settling her hands on her hips and managing a pretty decent glare. "I don't know what this *thing* between us is any more than you do, but I do know that I cannot be wondering about it when I walk into this party. You're *distracting* me, and you need to stop so I can focus on not making a fool of myself."

Would she ever stop impressing him? "How do you do that?"

Her glare got meaner. "Do what?"

Not the best way he could have framed that question, he realized too late. "You sounded like a lawyer—just like you did in Lenon's office."

She tried to give him what had to be her meanest look ever, but he could see the smile lurking underneath. "I don't know. He made me mad. I guess I forgot to be nervous."

Just as she'd done the first time he'd interviewed her. Of course, that also meant that he'd made her angry again. That she was right—again—and he wasn't.

"And don't apologize," she said, cutting him off before he could get the words out. "I doubt either of us are truly sorry."

That admission was enough to make him relax. She wanted him, but she was the bigger person here, the one able to rank her priorities and act on them accordingly. They still had to go to this damn party, but…Yellow Bird was onto something, and the plane didn't take them back to South Dakota until tomorrow afternoon. That left a lot of time to explore how *not* sorry either of them was. This was going to work out. Maggie wouldn't have to be on the stand, and he wouldn't have to be in violation of his ethics for being with her.

They just had to survive tonight first. "Good. I'm sure there's plenty to piss you off at this party."

She shot him one heck of a look—one that walked a so-fine-as-to-be-invisible line between irritation and attraction. "These are *your* people, you know."

"A fact I'm sure I'll be apologizing for all night long. Let's get this over with."

* * *

Maggie sat in the back of the cab the doorman had hailed. James was close enough to her that she could feel the warmth from his legs, but not so close they were touching.

Not thinking about it, she reminded herself. She wasn't thinking about the stunned look on his face when he'd seen her in this dress, or the way the touch of his mouth to her neck had almost made her knees buckle. She was pointedly not thinking about how James made her feel desirable and special and sexy all at the same time.

No, what she was thinking about was a viper pit. "Who else will be there?"

"My parents, of course."

Of course. Vipers. "I don't want any more surprises, James."

He sighed, a weary-sounding thing. "Alexander Carlson, former secretary of defense, currently works as a lobbyist."

"What else?" Because she knew there *had* to be something else. She felt as if everyone in this town was hiding something—and this from a woman who had lived with serious secrets.

"Serial adulterer," James said, making it sound like common knowledge. But he couldn't fool Maggie. She saw the way his hands clenched when he said it. "Partial to staff members. Always working the angle."

"I see." In other words—her words—the guy was a real jerk. "Your mother?"

"Julia Carlson—functioning alcoholic. Carries on affairs with gardeners and the like. Sits on the board of several nonprofits. Has a lot of family money—she uses that to keep Dad in line. Thinks she's better than everyone else in the world."

Maggie didn't know what she was supposed to say to that, because she couldn't think of anything good to say. "They sound like quite the pair."

"Dad won't walk away from her money, and Mom is not about to give up the perks of power." He gave Maggie a worried look out of the corner of his eye. "In other words, my father will try to grab your ass, and my mother will treat you like the hired help."

Yup. Plenty to piss her off at this party. And these were his parents. James had been nothing but kind—more than kind—to her, but she had to wonder how far the apple fell from the tree. Would James turn into his father, grabbing the bottoms of every woman he came into contact with? Was Maggie something more to him, or was she just the first domino in his long fall into debauchery? She pushed these nagging thoughts from her mind. She had a viper pit to negotiate. "Forewarned is forearmed. What else?"

He sighed while staring out at the passing lights of D.C. Maggie wanted to look, too, but she had too much else to think about. "Pauline will be there."

"The woman your mother wants you to marry?"

"The one." But he didn't elaborate.

Maggie let him sit before she asked, "Do I need to worry about her?" Because she was already worried. Although, honestly, she couldn't tell which part of Pauline she was most worried about—the part that was supposed to be with James, or the part that made Julia Carlson like her.

All those hours spent watching reality TV had her a little worried. She knew what "reality" women did at fancy cocktail parties. She had no idea if anything tonight would be real—or as manufactured as her favorite show.

"I don't know. Pauline was…" He really seemed to be struggling with the words. "We were friends. She can be sweet when she wants to. Her mother is friends with my mother, and those two decided we belonged together." He turned to look at her, and there it was—that lost look. "We dated on and off for years."

What had he said about the woman who'd married Tommy? The safety date. Maybe that's what this Pauline was—the safety wife.

Would she sense the connection that James and Maggie couldn't deny and move in for the kill?

Only one way to find out. The hard way.

"Anyone else?"

"A lot of the lawyers you met today, but they're going to be busy drinking and sucking up. Everyone else there will be some sort of power player—either someone Lenon owes a favor, or someone who owes him a favor. And they'll all be working their own angles."

Panic tried to worm its way into her belly. Viper pit, shark tank—these were places that people went into, but didn't come back out of.

She realized she was fiddling with the weighty necklace. They could still take it back, but she was getting used to the weight. It didn't bother her as much.

"Stay close to me," James said. "If anyone asks too many questions, ask some back—these are the kind of people who can't talk about themselves and their awesomeness enough."

"What about the alcohol?" Because it was a cocktail party. She didn't think she was too far out of line to assume there would be cocktails—especially not after watching Lenon down two stiff drinks inside of ten minutes.

"There'll be waiters walking around with drinks, but there'll also be a bar. We'll go to the bar, get you something safe. Then hold on to it—take small sips."

"You won't leave me, will you?" That was the panic talking. She hoped that someone would say something jerky and fast so she could dig up that angry woman who was good with words and forget the scared girl who was being used as chum.

"No," James said, leaning over and placing a smoldering

kiss on her cheek. The same heat that had nearly swamped her earlier tonight—hell, every time James had kissed her—rode roughshod over her body. She couldn't control the shiver. "I won't."

Fourteen

Maggie held on to James's arm as he escorted her past a fountain lit with blue spotlights and into the tavern named after George Washington—or Georgetown, she wasn't sure. All she knew was that the expensive smell of cigars hung around the room like a low ceiling. Men—and some women—in dark suits blended into each other, while other women glimmered like disco balls in short, sequined dresses.

The little black dress—tight as it was in the chest—had been the way to go. What had felt obnoxiously out of place in Rosebud's office back home fit right in here.

By the time she and James worked their way into the bar, it was closing in on ten—an hour after the party had supposedly started, but Maggie could see that they were part of a huge crush of people all arriving at the same time. She knew about Indian time, of course—where appointments were more suggestions than anything else. This was different—less a casual, get-there-when-we-get-there thing, more a collective agreement that late was fashionable.

James led her toward the bar, but they didn't make it.

"James, darling!" A screeching female voice cut through the small talk. Maggie saw a tall, rail-thin woman coming toward them. Everything about her—from her forehead to her bust to her demure red silk dress—screamed "professional," making guessing her age impossible. She carried a nearly empty highball glass in her hands. "There you are!"

"Julia," James said in a low voice before adding, "Hello, Mother."

"You awful boy—Desmond was supposed to bring you home! Where did you run off to?" Julia Carlson's eyes cut to Maggie's face, then to where Maggie was lightly holding on to James's forearm. Her eyes narrowed into small slits. "What's this? You didn't tell me that Rosebud was coming with you. Does her husband know?"

Oh, *hell,* no. And just like that, Maggie was mad. *Furious.* Damn, but it felt good. "Hello," she said in her iciest voice as she stuck out her hand. "I'm Maggie Eagle Heart, legal assistant to Rosebud Armstrong. How do you do?"

"Maggie, this is my mother, Julia Carlson. Maggie is helping me out with a case, Mother." Already, he sounded tired by the whole pretense—and they were only ten minutes into the evening.

"Oh, I'm so sorry." Julia looked at Maggie's outstretched hand before finally stooping to shake it. "You look so much like her, I couldn't tell you apart."

The claws were out awfully early, Maggie thought. She couldn't be sure, but it sounded as if James was groaning.

"Yes," Maggie agreed. "We all do look alike. I can see how that would be challenging for you."

James snorted. Julia at least had the decency to look surprised at this bold statement. "I meant no offense."

Maggie gave her the nicest mean smile she had. "I assure you, I took none."

Julia blinked one, two, three times before she turned all her attention back to James, angling her body so that she presented her shoulder to Maggie. The dismissal was crystal clear. "Darling," she said to James in the sort of stage whisper that was meant to be heard by other people, "we were expecting you at home. Alone."

"I don't know why. I didn't tell you I was coming in. We had a meeting with Lenon, and we're leaving first thing in the morning. This is a business trip."

Julia's lower lip stuck out in a practiced pout. "But we haven't seen you in so long, James, darling. Pauline misses you ever so much. I think it's time for us to announce your engagement. I'm sure your work out there in Montana is *very* important, but it's time to get on with the rest of your life."

What the heck kind of social black hole had she fallen into? Maggie wondered.

"South Dakota, Mother." James's tone made it clear that he'd had this conversation before. "You can't announce anything. I haven't asked Pauline to marry me."

"But you will." Julia glanced over her shoulder at Maggie, as if this part was specifically designed for her ears. "You love her."

"This is not the time or place for this conversation, Mother." James stepped around Julia and nodded his head toward the bar. "Shall we?"

Quick as a wink, Julia's hand flashed out and latched onto James's arm. "We're not done having this conversation, *darling*."

Maggie had to wonder if Julia Carlson was a mean drunk, or just plain mean. "It was lovely to meet you, Mrs. Carlson," she said in her most insincere voice. Then she walked away.

"Nice job," James said when they finally reached the long, polished bar.

"She's a piece of work." Maggie had to smile as she wondered what would happen if Julia Carlson were to ever meet Nan. The battle would be long and bloody, she decided, but she'd put money on Nan coming out on top.

"Tell me about it." He ordered a Scotch on the rocks and a Shirley Temple—in a martini glass—for her.

Maggie wouldn't have thought having a glass in her hand would make her feel better, but it gave her something to do. Another nervous thread unwound in her belly. "That's one. Where's your father?"

"I've found it's best not to ask that question," he muttered around his drink.

She and James took up residence at one corner of the bar. From this strategic position, they had a good view of the room without being in the middle of the crowd. James knew everybody's name. While he kept track of hundreds of conversational strands, Maggie noticed that he wasn't as comfortable as she figured he'd be. His shoulders stayed tense under his black jacket, his forehead was permanently etched with concentration, and his eyes kept darting around the room.

Because Julia's dress was red, Maggie easily kept track of James's mother. The woman flitted around like a moth. She touched men on the biceps while smiling and did a lot of that cheek-kissing with women who had the same-style forehead she did. Maybe they all had the same plastic surgeon.

Lenon nodded at James from across the room and raised his glass to Maggie, but he didn't come over.

Maggie shifted her feet. According to her toes, she'd been standing here nursing her faux drink for three days, but they'd probably only been here an hour. She didn't know how much longer she could take it, though. People ignored her the second they figured out that she had nothing to offer them. Her face hurt from all the fake smiling, and her hand was starting to cramp around the stem of her martini glass.

Plus, any angry adrenaline she'd marshaled for Julia Carlson had long worn off. Yes, she'd had two short naps today. She'd still been up since 4:00 a.m., her time. If she were still at home, she'd be curled up on the couch with a mug of chamomile tea, watching some show that made fun of people like this and laughing with Nan.

Of course, if she were at home, she wouldn't be with James.

While she debated asking him when they could leave, she caught sight of Julia throwing her arms around a supermodel. Maggie elbowed James and nodded toward the pair.

"Pauline," he whispered. "Here they come."

Dang it, Maggie thought. She wasn't up for another round of hatefulness. Especially not when Pauline was the most perfect woman Maggie had ever seen. Tall without being Amazonian, slender without being anemic, her caramel-blond hair floating in soft waves down to her bare shoulders. The gray satin dress was so tight that Maggie was certain Pauline couldn't be wearing any underwear.

When the pair of women got about ten feet away, Julia pulled up and rushed off in a different direction. Maggie had just enough time to realize the man she was heading for looked like an older, stouter version of James before Pauline reached them.

"James," the supermodel James was supposed to marry said as she kissed both his cheeks in rapid succession.

"Pauline, you look lovely," he said, his hands on both of her arms.

A jolt of jealousy shot through Maggie. James had held her like that—right before he'd taken her on the kitchen counter. He'd mentioned that he and Pauline had dated on and off for years. Maggie knew she had no right to be this jealous. She'd only known James for a few weeks, tops. But she was. Intensely.

The two of them looked at each other for a long moment before they turned to Maggie. "I'm Pauline Walker," she said, extending a manicured hand. She wasn't as condescending as Julia had been. In fact, she bordered on warm. "Nice necklace."

"Thanks. Maggie Eagle Heart." Was this the part of her that could be sweet? "Nice to meet you."

Pauline nodded and turned back to James. "Julia's quite upset with you."

"And that's news?" The two of them grinned. They acted more like the oldest of friends than current lovers. Maggie tried to relax. "How have you been?"

Pauline waved the words away as she opened her handbag and pulled out a cigarette and a lighter. "Busy. You?"

"The same." James lit her cigarette for her, a gesture that seemed more fitting to a Humphrey Bogart movie than Maggie's life. "You do know smoking indoors is illegal?"

"Like I care," Pauline said with a wave of her hand.

James didn't seem to fit in—not the James Maggie knew, anyway. She couldn't imagine that this was how he had grown up, but then she remembered—he'd had that nanny. Instead of going to parties like this, he'd spent his time with a woman who raised him as a son. No wonder he didn't seem entirely comfortable.

How did people live like this, going to parties where no one had fun and everyone had an agenda? How did people get married to keep the same system going? Maggie would have no part of it. This was not her world, and if she had anything to say about it, it never would be.

"James, darling!" Julia Carlson pushed in between Maggie and Pauline, which drove Maggie farther away from James while simultaneously moving Pauline closer to him. "Oh, it's so good to see you two together again. Don't you think so, Alex?"

"Of course," Alex Carlson said as he eyeballed Maggie's cleavage. She moved a step farther away—out of groping range. His suit was exquisitely cut, and he had a diamond pin anchoring his tie. His hair was the same color as James's, but there was less of it.

Ugh. Maggie wanted to go home and wash the stench of cigars and creepiness off her skin. She was sure she'd proven that she could handle a hostile environment to James and Lenon and the whole lot of them. Time to leave.

"No." James's voice suddenly cut through the chatter of the party like sharp steel through the air. "That's ridiculous."

"Now, darling," Julia said in a pleading voice as she glanced around the room. "Don't cause a scene."

Pauline took two mincing steps backward, nearly crushing Maggie's toes.

"You can do a better job here, son." Alex's voice carried an implicit threat.

"I'm in the middle of a *case,* Dad. I'm not going to pick up and move back home so you two can keep an eye on me. I'm a grown man, goddamn it."

"Now you listen to me," Alex roared.

"Dear!" Julia grabbed both of them by the arms and, with more strength than Maggie would have given her credit for, pushed toward a doorway. "People are *listening.*" And with that, she shoved them into a back room.

The door swung shut behind them. Maggie had no idea what she was supposed to do, because now she was alone with Pauline, who was working on her third cigarette.

"So," Pauline began, exhaling smoke like a busted chimney. "You and James, huh?"

"I don't know what you're talking about." Which was a lie, and they both knew it. Maggie debated squishing Pauline's toes and making a break for it—she was *so* done—but she couldn't do it. The woman had been the most pleasant person at this party.

Pauline shrugged, casting her gaze around the room. Maybe she was used to people telling bald-faced lies as a regular part of conversations. "He's a great guy. His mother is a bit much, though."

"Ah." Because what else was there to say? *Why would you want to marry into that?* That didn't seem appropriate. Nothing did.

Pauline's face lit up as she stared at something across the room. Maggie followed her gaze and saw a man watching the two of them. Well, he was watching Pauline, anyway. Something clicked, and Maggie realized that Pauline didn't want to marry James. Whoever was across the room was who Pauline wanted.

"You and James, huh?" It wasn't much for small talk, but there was nothing else, and she didn't want to talk about herself any more than necessary. Besides, she wanted to know what Pauline would say about James while she looked at that other guy.

Pauline sighed. "More like our mothers arranged a marriage when we were ten, and they've convinced themselves that we're the last two humans on the face of the earth." She gave Maggie an exhausted smile. "James's mother doesn't have the crazy market cornered, you know."

"So why do it?"

Pauline turned her full attention to Maggie. "Because, in my world, love is an unfortunate by-product, one that can be remedied by getting your heart broken a few times. Children are bargaining chips to be used. Happiness is not relevant. Power is everything. The only thing."

The sadness in her voice was familiar—too familiar. Maggie knew the feeling of having no control over your life, of being nothing more than a commodity for other people to use and abuse. Pauline was a beautiful woman, but she still let herself be used. And that made Maggie sad for her.

"Things can change," Maggie heard herself saying. "But only if you want them to." She'd said the same thing to James once. Maybe he believed it, maybe he didn't.

"Maybe I don't know what I want." Even as she said it, Pauline's eyes searched the room.

"Who is he?"

"No one important." With that blanket dismissal, Pauline ground out her cigarette into an empty glass.

Maggie was going out on a limb here, but what the hell. "What if James decides he doesn't want to get married?" She left off the "to you."

Anything "warm" about Pauline vanished. Her eyes cut back to Maggie with lethal efficiency. "You're obviously not from around here, so I'll give you a little tip." Her words came out with the same lethalness—machine-gun bullets hell-bent on cutting Maggie to shreds. "Men like James—like his father—don't love anyone. Not their wives, not their children, and most certainly *not* their mistresses. Don't be one of those sad, pathetic women who thinks they can *change* him," she said, making air quotes around the word, "because men like James *never* change. Certainly not for the likes of *you*."

And then she was gone, stalking away on her thin heels so fast that smoke-flavored air spun in little eddies after her. Her words swirled in the smoke, bouncing off each other until it seemed that the whole room rang with them.

The likes of Maggie? Had she been deluding herself into thinking that someone who came from this cat-and-mouse world, who was raised by people who valued appearances and power above all else—someone like *James*—could possibly love someone as poor and screwed up as her?

Certainly not.

Fifteen

"You're out of your mind." James wrenched free from his mother's iron claws and looked back toward the door. Damn it, Maggie was out there. Alone.

"James, it's time." Dad used his no-argument voice. "Bachelors may get elected to the House of Representatives, but hell, son—any idiot can do that. You have higher aspirations. If you want to go anywhere in this town, you have to have a wife."

That crap might work on deputy assistant undersecretaries, but not on James. Not since he was fourteen. "If you want a Carlson to be president that bad, Dad, *you* run."

"Look at Bill and Hillary, darling," Mother pleaded. Her approach was different, but no less annoying. "Think of what they've accomplished because they got—and stayed—married. Think of all the good you could do with Pauline by your side."

While they attempted to boss and persuade him, he worried about Maggie. Damn it all, he'd promised not to leave her alone out there.

"And I miss you," Mother went on, turning on the waterworks. James rolled his eyes. She only cried when she wanted something. He'd seen her break down everyone from art dealers to PTA moms with a few well-placed tears. It even worked on Dad, if she did it right. "You're my only child. I hope that I live long enough to see my grandchildren…" Her voice trailed off as she hid her muffled sobs behind her hands.

Oh, for God's sake. Even though he knew it was just another weapon in her arsenal of guilt, he still felt an irritating pang of responsibility. Quickly, he shoved it away. The last time he'd let her manipulate him like this, he'd agreed that marrying Pauline wasn't a bad idea. And see where that had gotten him? Trapped in a back room, being browbeaten by his parents. The only way to win this game was to refuse to play it. "Are we done yet? I've got a plane to catch in the morning."

"James, please!" Tears gone as quickly as they'd started, his mother was now glaring at him. "I don't know what you're trying to prove staying out there in that hellhole, but enough is enough. You're not doing your career any favors. Your place is in D.C., with your family—who loves you."

The awful thing was, she was serious. This twisted version of ownership *was* love to his parents. As if they had to prove its validity to themselves and the rest of the world, they demanded James replicate it.

He turned and began to walk away, but his father grabbed him by the arm and hauled him back with enough force that James almost lost his footing. "Your mother is right. Enough is enough. It's time to stop dicking around. I've already discussed it with Lenon. He'll be recalling you by the end of the month."

"You *what?*"

Dad's eyes glittered with a victory that left James cold.

"Your case is collapsing. Who cares about one old judge, any-way? It's not worth it. It's better to let the case die than risk the public humiliation of a loss. You'll receive a promotion, of course. It's been settled."

James gaped at the man. He'd pulled plenty of dirty tricks before—too many to count—but James had clearly underestimated the depths to which he would sink.

Having Lenon recall him to D.C.? After James had sat in the man's office today, wringing a green light out of him? Had it all been for show, then? Maynard would go free, no matter whether or not Yellow Bird's lead produced anything usable. And what would happen to Maggie? Her name had been handed over to the defense as part of discovery. He was responsible for her now, whether or not she testified, regard-less of his feelings for her.

His mother continued glaring at him. James couldn't re-member the last time he'd seen his parents in such agree-ment—and it was because he wasn't toeing the family line. He was looking at his future, he suddenly realized. He could talk about his father sleeping with female staffers, but the truth was, James had slept with Maggie. He could no longer claim the moral high ground. He'd pushed their relationship to that point, and if he came home to D.C., he'd never see her again. He'd marry Pauline and watch as she started sleep-ing with the help. How long would it be before James found himself growing fond of another underling, when faced with a wife who had never loved him? How long before he sac-rificed more of his morals for power? How long before he turned into his father?

No. If being a career politician meant that he sacrificed what he believed in, he wouldn't do it. The only way to win this game was not to play it.

The next thing James realized, he'd shoved his father. Hard. The old man stumbled back, the surprise writ large on his face. His mother gasped in real shock, but James didn't care. He was *not* playing this game anymore.

"You listen to me, both of you. I'm your *son,* not your pawn. I have a job and a life—and neither of them are here. I'll quit before I move home. I won't marry anyone just because you think it'll look good in the papers—least of all Pauline. *If* I run for office, it'll be because I want to, not because you tell me to. And you can be damn sure I won't be letting any children I may or may not have *near* you."

His mother made a strangled noise in the back of her throat before she came up, both barrels blazing. "We'll cut you off. You'll have nothing. You'll be *nothing.*"

"There are worse things in the world than being poor," he said, and in his head, he heard Maggie say that in her quiet, serious voice.

His mother was wrong. It wasn't money that made a person powerful. That kind of power was based on fear and jealousy. That power was temporary, liable to change with the next election. He understood that now. He'd always known that—felt it, deep in his soul—but he hadn't realized how wrong she was until Maggie had shown him that real power came from love. Real power didn't come from bending someone to your will, or from being bent. Real power came from the freedom to choose—to give yourself freely.

Your choice, he thought. Maggie had told him that, too. And to think, she'd tried to convince him she wasn't that smart.

He turned away from the two of them and walked. His father roared something demanding and insulting, but James didn't listen and he didn't stop. To hell with them. He had to find Maggie.

She wasn't where he'd last seen her, at the bar. Pauline was gone, too. Doom crowded around the anger in his stomach. He couldn't have been gone more than fifteen minutes—where could she be? Ladies' room, maybe? But something told him that wasn't the case.

"Have you seen the woman I was with?" he asked as he worked his way through the crush of people.

A few people shook their heads no, some shrugged, but most couldn't care less. No one remembered seeing the beautiful American Indian woman in the slinky black dress.

He made his way outside. Relief washed over him when he saw her standing by the fountain. Suddenly, he was tired. He'd forgotten how hard it was to play the mind games this place required. He wanted to go home—and he knew now that home wasn't here anymore. What he wouldn't give for a flight out of Dulles tonight, so he could get back to the wide spaces of South Dakota. Back where he could breathe without someone ascribing ulterior motives to his oxygen status.

Back where Maggie could be Maggie, not some fictional version of herself. Her eyes had a faraway look to them, as if she'd already gotten on that plane out of town. That feeling of doom got a little stronger. Pauline wouldn't have cut her down—would she? Maybe Maggie was just tired. It had been a long day, after all. He had to get her out of here.

"Maggie." She didn't react—not even a flinch—when he put his hand on the small of her back and guided her away from the fountain. "Let's go."

Silently, they got into a waiting taxi. It was still early for most partygoers, so the traffic wasn't horrendous. Maggie sat on her side, staring out the window.

She was obviously overwhelmed—hell, after that little chat with his parents, he was nearing overload, too. So he let her sit. He let himself sit, too.

His mind was a jumble. Perhaps it was the universal nature of parents to refuse to admit that their children had grown up into fully functional adults. He couldn't be the only person in the world whose parents wanted him to move closer to home.

Hell, he wasn't even the only person whose parents had delusions of higher-office grandeur. And Lord knew there were plenty of parents out there who had lost touch with reality.

He shouldn't let Alex and Julia Carlson get to him—but they did. And, given her silence, they'd gotten to Maggie, too.

If the case was dead, then Maynard would go free, damn it all. There would be no justice for Maggie or all the others like her. That bothered him. But if he knew Yellow Bird—and he liked to think he did—he knew that the FBI agent would keep digging whether the case was alive or dead. If he found something new, something that wouldn't drag Maggie back into this mess, James knew Yellow Bird would get it into the right hands. Just because James wouldn't personally get to put Maynard away didn't mean he was giving up on justice, even if it felt like justice—or at least the Department of Justice—was giving up on him.

But then he realized there was a bright side to this. With the case dead and Lenon recalling him, he *would* quit. He'd submit his resignation first thing Monday morning. He didn't need his parents' money. He had an excellent track record—it shouldn't be too difficult for him to get a job on his own. He wouldn't have Bentleys and drivers, but he didn't need that stuff anyway. He wouldn't be rich. But he would be free.

And once he was out, he no longer had to worry about compromising a witness. There would be no conflict of interest, nothing to compromise. He could be with whomever he chose, and after tonight, he knew that wasn't Pauline or anyone his mother might approve of. As the cab pulled up outside the hotel, he realized that he was free to be with Maggie—to love her, if that was what he wanted. The relief that came with this realization was so powerful that he broke out into a smile. Suddenly, the future looked a hell of a lot brighter. Because right now, he was pretty sure that loving Maggie was exactly what he wanted.

When they arrived at the hotel, he paid the driver and then offered Maggie his hand to help her get out of the cab. But he didn't let go once she was safely on her heels. Her hand was warm and soft against his. She was someone real and solid and honest, and right now, he needed to remember that those kinds of people did exist.

She didn't pull away as they walked across the hotel lobby, nor did she remove her hand from his in the elevator. James couldn't say if their silence was comfortable or not, but he didn't care. They headed down the hall to the hotel room—complete with multiple beds.

He held the door for her, then he let go of her hand so he could hang out the Do Not Disturb sign and throw the bolt. Whether he slept in his own bed or someplace else, having Housecleaning bust in on them was not how he wanted to start his morning.

When he turned back around, he saw that Maggie had walked over to the windows. Except for the bare skin of her legs, her black hair and black dress made it almost impossible to see her. As he watched, she took one, then another small step out of her shoes and kicked them away. But her focus remained out the window.

"Maggie?"

"It's so beautiful," she said in a low, awestruck voice as she stared out at the twinkling lights of his hometown. "Even better than in the movies."

He moved toward the window, trying to see what she saw. Just the bright lights of a big city. Something he took for granted, he guessed. He'd grown used to the absolute darkness of a moonless Pierre night, where no light pollution marred the twilight with its ugly red glow.

He got the feeling this wasn't about the view, though. So he waited, standing a few steps behind her.

She leaned forward, putting her palms flat on the glass.

"From up here, it looks…perfect. Clean and bright and smart. Not like home, where everything's always dusty," she added, sounding a little more like herself.

"But?"

"But…it's a trick. It's not real—like the necklace isn't real. I thought…" She leaned forward, her head resting on the glass. "I thought things might be different here, but they're not."

"What do you mean?"

"Oh, everyone's got money, that's different. Money and cars and clothes and houses. People here don't freeze to death in the winter or starve in the summer."

That was how she'd grown up. Rosebud had taken him through her reservation when he'd first come out to South Dakota, to show him how people out there had to live. It had been a hard thing to see, harder to know that someone he cared for had lived like that. But the hardest thing had been to know that he could have offered to take her away from that—brought her here to this world, with its money and cars and houses—and Rosebud would have refused.

Just as Maggie was doing right now. Refusing. She was making a choice—and that choice wasn't James's world.

"But how people *use* people—that's the same." She sighed, a sad sound full of a lifetime of disappointment. "People *let* themselves be used. I didn't think it would be like that."

Then she hit him square between the eyes with the shot he should have seen coming. "I didn't think *you* would be like that. I thought you were different."

Pauline. And his mother and father. And Lenon. The cumulative effect of the entire day must have led to one inescapable conclusion—that James was one of *them,* someone not to be trusted. He would give it all up for her, but that wouldn't change the fact that he would always be one of them.

No doubt, she couldn't love him.

He should turn around and go to bed. She'd clearly made up her mind, and he didn't have a defense ready. But he couldn't bring himself to leave her there, looking down on the sparkly world that hid humanity's ugliness.

He stepped in closer, wanting to touch her, to reassure himself that she was still really there. He saw the tension ripple down her arms and up to her flattened palms, but she didn't stop him as he put his hand on the small of her back, above the swell of her bottom. But that was all—a simple touch to remind him that she was a real, honest person.

Honest enough to tell him he wasn't.

"The thing I can't figure out, though, is why you're not like them." Her voice was down to a bare whisper. He had to lean in close to make out the words, smelling her clean scent under the dirty odor of cigars and lies. "Why aren't you like them?"

"Consuela. And Desmond, and other people like them—a few teachers in school, my softball coach. People who were real and honest and treated me like all the other kids instead of like the ruler of the world." He closed his eyes. He'd lost Consuela, that grounding force gone forever. But she wasn't gone as long as he remembered her and everything she'd taught him. "People who expected more of me. People like you, Maggie. You make me a better man."

For a moment, she didn't move, and James knew that even though he'd spoken the truth, he still wasn't good enough for her. But then she leaned back, the warmth of her body pressing into the side of his. They stood there, watching the D.C. lights twinkle under a rusty sky.

"I take it back." A warmth had crept into her voice, one that made him all kinds of hot. She leaned her head back onto his shoulder and turned her face into his neck. He felt her sweet breath blow away the last of the evening's frustrations. "You're not like them. You're better."

Sixteen

Better. Who knew that one word could have so much power over him? He couldn't disappoint her, not when she had so much faith in him. He was not going to rush this. This time Maggie would be properly seduced. She deserved to feel as special as she truly was. She deserved to feel loved.

The heady rush that came with the realization that he was in love with her—and that she loved him back—was enough to send his pulse racing. He felt as if ten years had been shaved off his life. This was how it was supposed to be, he realized. No complicated negotiations, no power plays. Just two people making things right.

So James forced himself to kiss her slow and deep. He tasted the sweetness of the Shirley Temple on her tongue—the taste of innocence, he thought. Maggie reached up and ran her fingers through his hair, pulling his mouth down harder onto hers.

Go slow, he told himself. If this didn't work, he was going to have to think about William Howard Taft again, and that wasn't nearly as much fun as thinking about Maggie.

The kiss got deeper. James felt his slow-and-steady resolve start to weaken. She was making her choice, and she was choosing him. After the hell he'd put her through, she was still choosing him. Emotion constricted his chest until he felt light-headed. She'd handled everything demeaning and conflicting and deceiving about his world with such strength and grace that he wasn't sure he was worthy of the gift of her affection.

She pulled away, and he was terrified that she'd read his mind—and agreed he wasn't worthy. But that wasn't it. Her eyelashes fluttered as her chest heaved. "We shouldn't."

"I'm going to resign my position on Monday, Maggie."

Her eyes widened as she turned to look at him. "You are? Why?"

"Because I finally figured out what I want, and it's not the power or the money. I can do good in this world without having to mortgage my soul. I want to be worthy of you, Maggie. I want to love you. That's all I really need."

"Are you serious?"

He couldn't help grinning at her, and her lips curved into a smile he couldn't read—relief? Disappointment? Excitement? Then he was kissing her again—still slowly, but with more urgency.

Tonight was the first night of the rest of his life, and he wanted to live it right—loving this beautiful woman in his bed.

The zipper didn't want to cooperate, but with more force than he intended, he yanked it down and almost pulled the whole dress right off her.

"Sorry," he mumbled against her mouth.

She giggled as he did what he'd wanted to do earlier. He slid his hands underneath the black fabric and pushed the dress off her shoulders. It slid over her hips with a shushing noise and hit the ground.

Whatever oxygen he'd been breathing got stuck in his throat at the sight of her back in nothing but a black bra and a matching thong. The wave of desire that hit him was so strong that it nearly brought him to his knees. He'd never been a thong guy—a woman wearing nothing was much preferred—but he was going to have to reevaluate his thinking on the matter. The sheer black fabric rode high on her hips before swooping between the nicest backside he could ever remember seeing.

He didn't want to just look, though. He ran his hands over her shoulders, moving her swath of silky hair out of his way. *Slow* was more of a guideline than a law, but he told himself that tasting each part of her body was going slow enough. He kissed the back of her neck at the base while his fingers ran ahead and stroked each muscle. Because she had muscles. Underneath the satin of her skin, tight deltoids rolled with desire as he touched them, proof that she wasn't afraid of hard work. He took his time appreciating each and every one of those earned muscles, which made him harder than he'd ever been.

Until he got to the tattoo that covered so much territory on her right shoulder. She unexpectedly shuddered, pulling away from him. "Don't. Not that."

As James shook some sense back into his head, he found himself wondering about that tattoo. She'd had her teeth and skin fixed—all except that scar on the side of her face and this tattoo. He ran a finger over the ink. "Why did you keep it?"

"Because." He thought that was the only answer he was going to get, but then she took a deep breath. "Because it cost a lot of money, and they couldn't promise it would go completely away."

He wasn't buying that answer. He stepped forward, trailing his finger down to her bra strap. As he unhooked it, he kissed the flames. "And?"

He slipped the straps of her bra off her shoulders. Finally, he could see those breasts, even if they were reflected in glass. The megawatt sparkle of her necklace shined between her breasts. Despite the scars and the tattoo, or maybe because of them, she was perfect. He slid his hands around her chest and cradled the full weight of each breast. Just touching—and appreciating—was one of the most sexually satisfying moments of his life.

"I was afraid I would forget who I'd been."

As his fingers stroked and tugged at her chocolaty-brown nipples, her bottom quivered against his zipper. James had to remind himself that tonight was all about showing her how much she was cherished.

"I needed to remember so I'd never fall into that trap ever again."

As loath as he was to relinquish his hold on one of her breasts, he let his hand slip down her waist and over the thin V of black fabric. She gasped as his fingers stroked lower and lower. "I will never forget who you are now, Maggie."

"Who am I?" Her breath was ragged. She needed him. And she trusted him.

He felt the tight nub of tender flesh beneath the panties. He began to rub in measured circles. "The honest, beautiful, intelligent woman I'm falling in love with."

Maggie's head fell back against his shoulder as she sucked in air while he tugged and rubbed and stroked and kissed, because he couldn't keep any part of him off every part of her. And through it all, he held her.

She laced her fingers through his hair as she arched her back. Oh, she was ready for him. Her whole body shaking, she ground down onto his fingers, her hips rolling from side to side as she gasped, "Oh, James!" over and over. He could feel her wet warmth through her panties. If he got any harder, he'd become a stone, a permanent reminder of the effect she had on him.

Suddenly, she turned her face to his. "Come, babe," he whispered as he kissed her.

With a cry of pleasure, she went limp against him. He spun her around and picked her up. He'd carry her to bed. That was the noble thing to do.

When she wrapped her legs around his waist, though, he was pretty sure she was going to be the death of him. Once she settled against him, he tried to move and didn't get far.

"Take me to bed, James." Her throaty whisper hummed through his blood until he couldn't tell what was noble from what wasn't anymore. Holding her in his arms had wiped away his past, his family, his ambitions. All that was left was her.

But he did as he was told. He picked his room—it had the suitcase with the condoms in it, and he didn't want to leave her side for so much as a moment.

Maggie was draped against him. "Are you sure?" he forced himself to ask when he got to his doorway.

She nodded, her head resting on his shoulder. "I trust you, James."

That was all he needed to hear. It was hard to be careful and quick at the same time, but it didn't take long before he had her down on the bed.

He ached at the sight of her spread out before him. Luckily, she didn't stay that way for long. She pulled herself up to her knees and grabbed his tie. With far more concentration than he was capable of, she undid the knot, removed his jacket and unbuttoned his shirt. But when she made a move for his belt, he had to stop her.

The condom. Yeah, that was what he needed to remember. He took a couple of slow breaths as he dug one out, and then took care removing his own pants. Maggie's smile was on the coy side of shy, but she didn't avert her eyes as he rolled on the protection.

He knelt on the bed and reached for her panties. The thong had looked damn fine on, but even better off, where he could finally see the curls of glossy black hair that covered her sex.

"Oh, Maggie." That was the full extent of his pillow talk as she fell back onto the bed, pulling him with her. Any attempt at slow was now a memory as his body found her center all by itself. As he slid into the welcoming embrace she offered him, he kept his eyes open.

She watched him the whole time their bodies moved together, her eyes wide in reverent wonder as she took and gave. She stroked his chest, his back, her every move like a prayer. She looked as if this was the first time she'd been with someone who cared for her the way he did—maybe it was. That thought strengthened his resolve to do right by her tonight.

He wasn't going to last much longer. It didn't seem possible that only three days had passed since he'd been with this woman. The space between that release and this one felt like a lifetime, maybe longer. How could she do that to him— make him need her so much? Because he did. He needed her.

He couldn't keep his mouth off her. Her body tensed around his, draining the last of his self-control. *Amen,* he thought as his climax ripped through him. They were coming together. They *belonged* together.

That feeling didn't fade when he pulled himself off her, nor did it lessen when they went to their separate bathrooms. If anything, it got stronger when she slid under the covers with him and pressed her body along the length of his.

She was going to stay with him. As he drifted off into an exhausted, yet satisfied, sleep, he tried to think of the last time a woman had stayed all night. Rosebud never had. Same with Pauline, except maybe a time or two.

As he faded, he felt himself hug Maggie tighter as he turned and kissed the top of her head. She leaned up and pressed her lips to his.

This, he thought as he slipped off into the black, *was happiness.*

Seventeen

Maggie awoke with a start. For a terrifying second, she couldn't remember where she was. She couldn't recall having ever seen this bed or these walls before. Where were her walls? Where was Nan? Where were her *clothes?*

Before panic could take over, she took a deep breath, and James's scent rushed over her, bringing with it the memory of foreplay and lovemaking. Of feeling safe and falling asleep.

Other memories came with those, faster than she could handle them. Ice-cold parents and an angry Pauline. Early mornings and bumpy plane rides. Being ignored and insulted.

None of that mattered, she reminded herself. James—how he made her feel, how he treated her—that was what mattered.

Ugh, her head hurt. She looked around for a clock. Holy cow, it was 10:23. That seemed late, but then, she had no idea when she'd gone to sleep. Maybe it was early.

She was alone in this room. James's room. Where was he? He hadn't bailed on her, had he? One way to find out. The only thing of hers in here was her underwear. An unusual self-consciousness gripped her, and she decided there was no way in hell she was going to parade around this hotel room in her skimpiest panties. No way, no how.

Which didn't leave her with a lot of options. She slipped on her underthings and then grabbed James's button-down shirt from the floor. Better than nothing.

She cracked the door open, feeling nervous for reasons she couldn't quite grasp. The smell of fresh coffee and bacon filled the small hallway, reminding her that she hadn't had real food since that quick dinner almost sixteen hours ago.

The low hum of someone saying something they didn't want anyone else to hear mixed in with the smell of breakfast. James was talking to someone.

She took quiet steps out of the room. An almost-full coffeepot was on the kitchenette counter. Next to that stood a wheeled cart with domed plates on it. Another step, then two, and she saw him. He was standing in front of all those windows, talking on his cell phone. He wore his suit pants and nothing else.

He was still here. That made her feel better. No one had ever stayed a whole night with her before.

"Okay. See you then." James hung up and immediately dialed again.

Maggie shouldn't listen. Eavesdropping was not a good idea. But who would he see? And when?

James stood with his back to her. Good Lord, what a nice back it was. Broad and muscled—more muscles than she would have guessed a lawyer would have. His beltless pants sat low on his hips, and for some reason, Maggie decided he looked as if he was doing a photo shoot for some lawyer-themed beefcake calendar—"Lawyers Debriefed" or something ridiculous like that.

"Hey, it's me." Against her better judgment, Maggie continued to listen. Who was he calling while he thought she was still asleep? "Yeah, I've missed you, too. It's been hard."

She was not going to jump to conclusions. He could be talking to anyone. Anyone who would know him by voice alone. Anyone he would miss—and who would miss him back. Yup. Could be anyone. Surely he wasn't talking to a lady friend after spending the night with her. Right?

"I know, but—no, I—Pauly, listen to me."

Oh. Pauly. Pauline. *Oh.*

Maggie started to back away as Pauline's parting shot rang in her ears. Men like James didn't love their wives, children or their mistresses. Where did that leave Maggie? Last night, James had sweet-talked her with the promise that he was quitting his job, and she'd fallen right into bed with him. Maybe she wasn't as smart as she thought she was. Maybe he'd just manipulated her—used her—the way Pauline had said he would. He wouldn't do that to her.

Would he?

"Look. I called to tell you we can't keep this charade going. It's over. It never really started."

Maggie froze, unsure if she could trust her ears. Was he *dumping* Pauline?

"No, I'm not alone, and let's be honest, neither are you." He paused, and then sighed wearily. "No, she didn't say anything. It's an educated guess. You're not waiting on me any more than I'm waiting on you. I don't care what Mother says."

Hope bloomed in Maggie's chest, squashing all those weedy little jealous spikes. He'd made his choice. He was choosing her.

"It's better this way. I have a chance to be happy, Pauly. I'm going to take it. I hope you take one, too."

He listened for a few moments while Maggie did her best not to laugh out loud. A chance to be happy. That's all it was, which, to her, didn't sound like much. She'd been happy enough with Nan—safe, well-fed, busy. Oh, no, this was different. A chance to be loved.

"You can tell her anything you want. I'm not coming back to D.C., so if you want to blame me, go for it. I'll take the heat." He made a snorting sound. "I'm used to it."

Maggie must have made a noise, because James spun around and caught her listening. *Busted.* His surprise was quickly replaced by a snarky grin. "I wish you the best, Pauly, you know that. Yeah. You do that. And if you ever need anything out west, look me up."

He hung up and stood there, looking at her. Which was fine, because she was looking at him. Who would have guessed that a lawyer could be so hot?

"I didn't hear you get up, beautiful."

Oh. My. Gooey warmth uncurled in her belly, temporarily blocking out the hunger. "I missed you."

"How long have you been standing there?"

If this were a movie, Maggie would have some camera-ready quip, like "long enough," ready to go. But her life wasn't a movie. Never had been, and wasn't about to start being one now. "I heard you call Pauline."

He nodded. "I gather she didn't leave you on the best of terms."

"She said…" Part of Maggie's brain screamed for her to shut up. James was going to take a chance on her. Maybe happiness was possible, maybe it was just a pipe dream—but right now, she didn't care. That chance, however unreal, was something she would hold near and dear for the rest of her life. Repeating Pauline's words could bring reality crashing back down on her head.

"She said that men like you and your father don't love your wives, your children or your mistresses."

James nodded again, as if this was common. Before he spoke again, he went over and poured two cups of coffee.

"She's half-right. Men like my father don't. But I'm not my father. And you're not my wife, my child or my mistress."

He seemed cool about this whole thing, while Maggie was a mess of emotions. Which had to be why she said, "What am I?" *Out loud.*

James walked over and handed her the cup. She took it with both hands, in case she developed a severe case of the shakes in the next thirty seconds or so. Then he traced the line of her cheek. "You're something else, Maggie. And I'm working on what that means."

He kissed her cheek, then her lips. Pure desire rushed through her, but then he stopped. "Breakfast first, then Desmond is coming at twelve-thirty to drive us around town."

Breakfast wouldn't take two hours, which meant... She must have blushed because he kissed her again. "We've got all the time in the world, beautiful."

Oh, she could get used to this.

After breakfast, they went back to bed for an hour. The sex wasn't frenzied and it wasn't slow. To James, it felt different than anything he'd ever shared with a woman. He was no saint. He'd had girlfriends and lady friends. But looking back, he had had few serious relationships that he'd acknowledged in public. The thing with Rosebud had always been hush-hush, and because he and Pauline had never been in love, they hadn't made a big public deal when they did date.

This, he thought as he held Maggie's shivering body and kissed her soft lips, *is serious.*

By the time Desmond showed up, both James and Maggie were showered and dressed. She'd wound her hair back into a simple braid and had forgone most of her makeup, but James had trouble remembering when she'd been more stunning. Gone was the tension that made her nervous and defensive. Yesterday's retreat into silence was long forgotten.

What was left was her sense of wonder and amazement. He noticed that Maggie couldn't stop smiling, and he liked it. He liked the feeling of having done right by her. Sure, it had taken a few days of missteps and trials by fire, but finally, he was taking care of her.

James knew Desmond noticed immediately, but the man's training wouldn't let him make a comment on the situation. Instead, he shot a conspiratorial wink at James and loaded up the bags.

"I'm surprised Mother let you come," James said to the older man when they were in the car.

"After last night, I made myself scarce this morning before she got up."

"She's furious, though, right?"

Desmond nodded. "I expect you'll be disowned before it's all said and done."

Maggie gave James a look that reminded him he hadn't had the chance to fill her in on the details. So while Desmond drove them to all the big landmarks, James explained that the case was dead despite their best efforts, no matter what Yellow Bird turned up.

"Which means we don't have to worry about compromising witnesses, right?"

James took her hand and ran his thumb over her knuckles. "I can't believe you once tried to convince me you weren't smart enough to be a lawyer." He also couldn't believe he'd tried to convince himself that he wouldn't get involved with her.

It was the fastest tour of D.C. on record. Desmond pulled up on the curb in front of this memorial or that monument, then James and Maggie bolted out of the car, had Desmond take their picture with Maggie's cell-phone camera and then ran back to the car.

He felt a tinge of nostalgia as they posed in front of Congress. He didn't know when he'd be get back to D.C. When would he again wander through all the Smithsonian museums or sit on the steps of the Lincoln Memorial and eat lunch? But any remorse he felt was forgotten when he looked at Maggie. Her eyes sparkled with wonder. Her enthusiasm was infectious, and James let himself get swept up in her excitement. For once, he didn't game plan tomorrow or next week or even next year. He enjoyed this moment of happiness. Whatever happened tomorrow, he was glad he'd taken the chance today.

By the time Desmond dropped them off at the airport, James had sweat through his shirt and Maggie's braid had come undone. Her camera had forty-two pictures on it. Forty-two images that showed him and Maggie grinning like idiots with their arms around each other's waists, in full view of the public. She hugged Desmond when he left, then took James's outstretched hand as they walked into the terminal.

He couldn't remember having more fun.

When they disembarked from the plane in Minneapolis, however, Maggie got quiet. "We should take it back," she said as she fingered the weighty necklace that peeked out from her shirt collar.

"You keep it. A souvenir."

"But it was so expensive—and if you change jobs…"

James wrapped his arm around her shoulder and pulled her hand away from the necklace. She was worried about him. It was sweet—and completely unnecessary. "I'll be fine, trust me. And every time you wear them…" He let his voice trail off as he kissed her just below her ears. Every time she wore that necklace and those earrings, he'd think of bringing her to a shaking orgasm with the lights of D.C. sparkling below them.

She was thinking the same thing. He could tell by the blush that dusted her cheeks, which matched the coy smile she shot him. "Okay." Then she frowned. "What are we going to tell Rosebud?"

That particular problem had been bothering him, too. "The truth. If she hasn't already, she'll figure it out sooner or later. She won't be as mad about us possibly ruining the case if we're up front."

"And Nan?"

"That's for you to decide, sweetheart. I imagine that she'll figure it out when she sees the pictures." Lost in her own thoughts, Maggie nodded as they strolled around the airport mall, looking at nothing in particular. "I would think she'll be happy for you," James added, hoping that was the case. The last time he'd seen Nan, she'd looked as if she was a short second away from wringing his neck.

The rest of the trip was uneventful. He gave Maggie a slow goodbye kiss in the Pierre airport parking lot. Part of him—the below-the-belt part—didn't want to let her drive the long road home. That part wanted to take her back to his apartment and spend the rest of the night and a good part of the morning readjusting to a South Dakota frame of mind.

But he hadn't resigned yet, so he reined in his desire and, with one more hug, sent Maggie home with a promise that he'd call her tomorrow. He leaned against his car and watched until her taillights disappeared, and even after she was gone, he couldn't stop grinning like a fool.

It had been a long time since he'd been in love.

He wanted to go home, but he'd given in to enough wants in the last twenty-four hours. Instead, he headed toward the office. He had a letter of resignation to compose and he wanted to make sure that he left everything in order for his successor. He'd need to write Agnes a letter of recommendation, just in case.

Lost in thought about the various career options open to former special prosecutors, James barely noticed the other car in the lot. Someone else working late, he thought as he headed in. But when he saw the light flooding out of his office into the darkened hall, he paid a lot more attention. Agnes was a top-notch legal assistant, but the last time James checked, it was still a Saturday night. Something was wrong.

"No, nothing—but I'll keep trying!"

At the sound of Agnes panicking, James broke into a dead run. He burst into the office as she hung up her phone. "What's wrong?"

"You're here! Where have you been? Why isn't your phone on? Where's Maggie?" She grabbed the phone and hit Redial.

The words spilled out of her so fast that they all ran together. But James understood the part about Maggie. "What's wrong, Agnes?" Stark terror ripped through him. "What about Maggie?"

"He's here—you tell him." Agnes thrust the phone out to him.

"Hello?"

"Where's Maggie? Tell me you've got her with you." Yellow Bird was shouting. James had never heard Yellow Bird panic before, not even when his wife died.

Remain calm, James tried to tell himself. It didn't work. "She's going home—we just got in, and she's driving home. Would one of you tell me what the hell is going on?"

Yellow Bird swore something in Lakota—not that James understood him, but the tone was unmistakable. "Leonard Low Dog is out," he said.

Oh, no. No, no, *no.* "When?"

"Yesterday."

"Who?" Because even through the gut-clenching terror and fire-hot rage, James knew instantly that this wasn't an accident. Low Dog had been nowhere near parole. He hadn't been released—someone had let him out.

Someone who wanted Maggie out of the picture.

Focus, James screamed at himself. *Focus on what's important.* "Where is he? Where are you?"

"That's the problem—I was checking on that lead down at field office in Omaha and didn't find out until about two hours ago. I just hit Sioux City—but I can't get there fast enough. And *you* haven't answered your phone."

"Damn it, I turned it off for the flight." He did some quick math. "She's got a half-hour head start."

"You better get there first, Carlson. Turn on your damn phone." The line went dead.

And James was gone.

Eighteen

The lights were out. She was thankful that Nan had already gone to bed—Maggie knew she smelled of James and airplanes. Even though she'd spent the whole two hours in the car trying to figure out how to tell Nan she'd fallen in love with James and she wanted to take a chance at happiness with him, she was still terrified of sitting face-to-face with the woman and saying the words out loud. Maybe it would all sound…stupid when she said it out loud. Like James would ever really give all that up for her.

She didn't want to go down that path—not now, not ever, and certainly not with Nan. She just needed a shower and some sleep. She'd know what to say in the morning.

Yeah. Right.

Something about the darkened house seemed…off. Nan hadn't left the porch light on for her. Surely Nan didn't think Maggie was coming home tomorrow—did she? Hell, if that was the case, Maggie could have given in to the temptation of one more night in James's arms. Because those arms were tempting.

Boy, one night in D.C., with all those bright lights, and she was already twitchy about the dark. She must be tired.

It wasn't until she shut the Jeep's door and started walking toward the house that the hairs on her arms and neck shot straight up. The air had a stale smell, like fear mixed with B.O. Maggie froze. The dark wasn't making her twitchy— someone was out there.

Then that someone stepped out of the shadows. "Look at you, baby girl," a gravelly voice hissed out of the night. "Looking real good, all clean and pretty, ain't you?"

Maggie died a little inside because she knew that voice. It was etched across the darkest parts of her memory, tangled up in cobwebs of shame and pain.

Leonard Low Dog was here.

Every one of her worst nightmares took another step toward her. Low Dog was still twenty feet away, but Maggie felt as if he'd already hit her in the face with the beer bottle again. She hadn't thought she could move, but her hand snaked up under her hair to feel the old scar tissue. No blood. She wasn't down yet.

As she realized that, Maggie felt a surge of strength. Was she scared right now? Oh, yes. Low Dog was every horrible thing that had ever happened to her all rolled into one rank body. Was she going to hide and whimper and beg for mercy?

Hell, no.

"What did you do to Nan?"

Low Dog took a step to the left. He was trying to flank her toward the house and away from the car. Like Maggie would leave Nan here to die. Maybe the old Maggie would have been every woman for herself, but she wasn't that woman anymore.

"Don't worry your pretty head about the old lady. She's taking a nap."

In her mind, Low Dog had always been this big, hulking man with hands of steel that towered over her. Now, though, he was about the same height as she was. The hulking part was a gut that made him look like he'd gone months past his delivery date. Why had she been so terrified of him? He was an ugly little man.

Where was James? He'd promised to tell her if Low Dog got out—and that hadn't happened. What was going on? God, if her heart beat any faster, she was going to have a heart attack. What she needed was a plan. She wasn't about to take whatever he was in the mood to dish out.

The shotgun in the umbrella rack. She'd tucked it back in there—could it really have only been a few days since James had been here? Surely Nan wouldn't have moved it—but had she tried to get to it? If she had, Low Dog would be swinging around a long barrel.

He took another menacing step. Screw it. If she couldn't get the gun, she'd have to hit him with a lamp or something. "I swear to God, *Leonard,* if you hurt that woman, you'll never be dead enough."

Low Dog snarled at her, which made Maggie smile. He'd never been a huge fan of the name Leonard. She liked that she could irritate him. A mad Low Dog was a careless Low Dog.

"Can't wait to taste your sweetness again, baby girl. Remember the first time? You were how old? Fourteen? And you cried when I was done. *So* sweet. That's a memory that's kept me warm on a lot of cold prison nights."

Ugh. Maggie shuddered with revulsion. She was in danger of letting him distract her, sucking her down to his level.

But she wasn't that same lost little girl anymore. She knew better now. She knew how to fight. "I was fifteen, *Leonard.* And you're a dirty old man. You can't hurt me."

"Wanna bet?" Low Dog lunged at her, but he'd slowed

down a lot in prison. Must not have been one of those guys in the weight room, she thought as she scooted out of his reach.

He sprawled out in the dirt, but didn't stay down. Maggie raced toward the house. She shoved the door open and fell inside. Actually, she fell over Nan.

"Nan! Are you okay?" But she got no response. The older woman's hands, feet and mouth were bound with shiny duct tape. Blood was matted into her hair and her eyes were closed.

Maggie wanted to scream. She couldn't bear to see Nan—good, sweet, kind, loving Nan—trussed up like a pig for slaughter. This wasn't how things were supposed to go. This was supposed to be the safest place in the world, tucked away under a hill in the middle of nowhere. Bad things weren't supposed to happen anymore.

"Trapped now, baby girl! No way out of that house. I'm gonna make that old cow watch, then I'm gonna make you watch what I do to her."

Hell, no. She wasn't going to let that happen. She'd die first.

She'd taken her chance at happiness—more happiness than she'd ever thought she'd get a shot at. She'd been loved—cherished—by a good man. She'd seen the sights in the nation's capital. She'd flown in an airplane. She could die defending her home and her family and not regret missing a thing.

Nan was still alive—she had to remember that. Dead people didn't need to be duct-taped. Now it was up to Maggie to keep her alive.

She scrambled back as Low Dog flipped on a light and came through the door. He was trying to herd her back into one of the bedrooms, but to go back was certain death. She blinked in the sudden light, but then so did he.

Her first instinct was to retreat—the kitchen. Knives. But Low Dog snatched that thought away from her. He gave Nan a small kick before he stepped over her. "She tried to cut me with one of them fancy knives you got in there. Got in a pretty decent shot." He held up his arm, and Maggie saw the rust-red that ran all the way down his sleeve. "Not much beats a frying pan to the head, though."

At least Nan hadn't gone down without a fight. "Too bad she missed your neck." Low Dog took another step toward her. In the light, he was even uglier than she had guessed. Someone must have used his face to mop the floor in prison a few times.

Maggie stood her ground until she could see around him. There—yes, the shotgun was still sticking out of the umbrella rack. When he took another step in, she scooted right, bumping into the couch.

"You can run, but you can't hide," Low Dog sneered at her.

"Really? That's the best you can do? Obviously didn't spend too much time reading in prison, did you, *Leonard?*"

"Stop that!" For the first time, Maggie heard uncertainty in his voice. He wasn't the big, scary man who'd held her hostage for five years. Maybe he was starting to realize she wasn't the same scared little girl anymore, either.

"What—that name reserved for all those big men in prison who made you their girlfriend? 'Oh, *Leonard,*' 'Yes, *Leonard,*' 'Harder, *Leonard.*' That's how it went down, isn't it, *Leonard?*"

When he lunged, Maggie was ready. She spun to the left, grabbed the lamp and swung.

She didn't miss, exactly, but she didn't hit him on the head. More like the shoulder. At least that was the arm Nan had done a little collateral damage to. Low Dog let out a furious roar as he went down over the back of her chair.

She leaped onto the sofa, but didn't quite stick the landing because Low Dog grabbed hold of one of her ankles. "Ow!"

"Got you!"

As she went down, her hand caught the lip of the umbrella rack. She landed in a heap on top of Nan, who groaned in pain. Still alive, Maggie thought as the umbrellas spewed out. Gotta keep it that way. Where the hell was the shotgun?

"You can't escape, baby girl." Hand over hand, Low Dog was pulling her back toward him. "You're mine. You always were. Damn shame to kill you, though."

She took what she could get. Maggie swung an umbrella and clipped him in the neck. "The feeling isn't mutual."

He snatched the umbrella away from her and backhanded her across the cheek. Darkness danced at the edge of her vision, the pain mixing with panic.

She'd never wanted to hear the sound of tires crunching on gravel more in her entire life, but she knew no one was coming. Maybe Low Dog would let her go if she threw up on him. Might be worth a shot if she couldn't get her hands on that damn shotgun.

"I *will* mess up that face again, baby girl. Ain't no one gonna think you're pretty when I'm done with you." He had her by both legs now. Apparently, he wasn't familiar with the concept of buttons or zippers, because he was yanking at the legs of her pants.

If she got out of this alive, Maggie made a mental note to thank Rosebud for buying quality clothing. The pants held.

"Hey, wake up, bitch!" Low Dog kicked at Nan, and in that second of diverted attention, Maggie felt her hand close around the polished wood of the shotgun butt.

Not dead yet.

She swung the barrel around at the same instant that Low Dog turned back to her. "What the—" Before he could finish his last thought, she pulled the trigger. The blast shook the walls, and Nan screamed behind the tape.

The butt kicked back on Maggie with a bite—she hadn't had time to get her shoulder into it, and she felt a bone snap on her right side. Low Dog jerked backward and crumpled to the ground over her ankles.

She didn't bother to see if he was alive or not—she didn't care, as long as he stayed down. She kicked him off her and then crawled over to Nan.

The whites of Nan's eyes were all Maggie could see. "Nan? Come on, Nan," Maggie pleaded as she pulled the tape from her mouth. But the older woman didn't react. "Nan?"

"Somebody, help me!" she screamed as she jerked at the tape around Nan's hands. She knew it was pointless—the only person who might hear her was Low Dog, and he wasn't going to be in a helping mood, but she couldn't stop herself from screaming. She tried to lift the older woman up—if she could get her to the Jeep—but her broken parts failed her. The pain was intense, and she had to let go of Nan. It was all she could do to shout out "Help!" one more time before darkness began to lick at the edge of her vision.

Lights shone through the open door. A car door slammed. A voice called out, "Maggie? Maggie!"

Someone had come. Someone would save her.

Then the world went black.

Nineteen

"Wake up." The voice was distant, but Maggie was sure she'd heard it before. "Wake up, sweetheart."

This time, she felt someone rubbing her hand. That was weird. If Nan was trying to get her out of bed, she'd just throw open the door and start shouting.

When the voice said, "Come on, Maggie. It's time to wake up," again, she also heard a pinging beep in the background.

That wasn't her alarm clock, and it wasn't Nan. She didn't know where she was, and that freaked her out. She tried to sit up, but a kaleidoscope of pain blossomed on her right side. She screamed, but it came out as a muffled groan instead.

"Easy, Maggie. Don't move. Just relax." Then the hand left hers and she heard the first voice talking to a second, female voice.

What the hell was going on? Relaxing was not an option right now, but panicking wasn't working for her, either. She decided to focus on getting her eyes to open. Then she could figure out where she was and what was going on.

"I'll increase her dosage," the second voice said.

"That won't compromise her sobriety, will it?"

"No, she'll be fine."

Compromise? Only one person used that word so regularly. James was here—wherever *here* was.

Boy, her eyes were in no mood to open, but a few seconds later, the pain in her arm dulled a little. Maggie was able to get both eyelids up at the same time. Progress.

What she saw was a colorless wall, which matched the colorless bed she was in and clear tubes that were attached to her hand. Her head decided to start throbbing again. She was in the hospital.

"How are you feeling, sweetheart?" James—for it really was him—leaned over and took hold of her hand again.

James. He was here. That was good. But why was everything so hard? Then her brain put one and one together. She was in the hospital, and the dosage—that was some sort of painkiller. She was on drugs. The panic got a little harder to fight. "Drugs?"

"You had to have surgery on your shoulder, so you're going to have to take something for a little while. The doctors have assured me you're in no danger of relapsing."

Maggie's eyelids fluttered, and she desperately wanted to shut them and slip back off into the comfortable dark. But she didn't. Surgery—on her shoulder. Her mind churned to remember why that was. She looked at James, hoping that he would give her a clue. The lines around his eyes seemed deeper now, making him appear worried and tired. He had a pretty aggressive five-o'clock shadow. When had he last shaved?

While she struggled to remember, another part of her relaxed. James was here. He wouldn't let anything bad happen to her. He'd promised.

In that moment of calm, the whole thing—Low Dog, Nan bound and gagged, the shotgun—all came crashing back to her. She jerked again, but James's hands were on her, holding her steady and making sure she didn't hurt herself.

"Nan…"

James gave her a weak smile. "Nan's fine. She's got a mild concussion and a few cracked ribs, but after a few weeks, she'll be as good as new. They sent her home last night. You saved her, Maggie."

"Low Dog?" Even saying his name hurt, like grinding salt into a fresh wound. Part of her wanted him to be dead, because that was the only way she would know for certain that he'd never hurt her again.

But if he were dead, that would mean she had killed him, and she didn't want to add murder to her list of crimes. Once, a long time ago, she would have killed him and not felt even a little bad about it. But she wasn't that person anymore. She didn't want to ever be that person again.

James wrapped her up in a big-yet-careful hug. "You did a damn fine job winging him, but he's alive. Yellow Bird is guarding him in Intensive Care. I'm going to do everything in my power to make sure he never leaves prison again."

It had been a good day to die, but it hadn't been her day. Relief choked her up, and the next thing she knew, she was blubbering. James didn't look at her like she was insane, though. Instead, he got a box of tissues and then came around to her good side and half sat on the bed and wrapped his arms around her as delicately as he could.

"I was waiting," she finally got out. "I was waiting for you to come and save me."

James's eyes got that wet, shiny look about them, and he

kissed her forehead. "You saved yourself, Maggie. Never forget that."

They sat like that for some time until Maggie had calmed down. Finally, she got to the point where she could say, "Now what?" without choking up.

James laced his fingers with hers, careful to avoid the IV tubes. "That's what I want to talk to you about. I promised to move you—new name, new place, at no cost to you—if you wanted. Remember?"

Maggie was going to nod, but then thought better of it. "Yes, but—" She had just found James. She didn't want to have to leave him so soon, not before they'd actually taken that chance at happiness.

"I want to give you that. New last name, new place." He paused, and she felt an odd tension in his hand. "I want to ask you to come with me when I get a new job. I want to ask you to marry me."

"What?" Maybe she was on more drugs than she thought—because he couldn't be asking her that. Could he?

"Happiness is next to me, Maggie. The fortune cookie said so. Nan already gave me her blessing." When Maggie didn't say anything for a stunned second, he hurried to add, "You don't have to answer right now. I know you're in a lot of pain..."

"You talked to Nan?" How long had she been out of it?

"I have a chance to be happy with you, Maggie, and it has nothing to do with winning cases or elections. I don't need any of those things to be a success. I realized that if I kept going down that path, I would never be happy because I would never be the kind of man you could love." He stroked her cheek. "I want to be the man who is worthy of you, sweetheart. I'm not going to let that chance slip though my fingers again. I love you." He pressed his lips to her forehead. Not a true kiss, but something that was tender and sweet and honest all the same.

All Maggie could do was lie there with her eyes closed and melt inside. This was what people meant by happily ever after. She'd saved herself and Nan. She was in love with a good man, and he loved her back.

"Let's start over together," James said, folding her good hand into his. "Marry me."

A new name and a new place—a new life with this man who would love and cherish her for the rest of his life. It was her choice. She was in control of her own life, and she could do whatever she wanted. Whatever would make her happy.

"I choose you, James. I love you."

Epilogue

"Hey, Yellow Bird, did you see this?" Hughes slapped a newspaper down on Tom's desk. "Can you believe that?"

The big man's gut was intruding into Tom's personal space. He leveled a look at Hughes, who promptly took two steps back. Satisfied, Tom turned his attention back to the newspaper. It was the lifestyle section from yesterday's Sunday paper, filled with engagement, anniversary and wedding announcements.

Hughes had folded it so that only one photo was visible. "Thought Carlson was married to the job."

Tom ignored Hughes as he skimmed the article. Eagle Heart/Carlson, the title read.

"Miss Maggie Eagle Heart wed James Carlson at the Brown County Courthouse in Aberdeen, South Dakota, on September 20, 2013. The bride was given away by her grandmother, Nanette Brown. The bridegroom is the son of Julia and Alexander Carlson, former secretary of defense. The ma-

tron of honor was Rosebud Armstrong. Best man was Dan
Armstrong. Also in attendance was Agnes Brock. The bride
is the owner of Eagle Dancer Designs, a successful Native
American jewelry-and-crafts business. The bridegroom is a
graduate of Georgetown University and was recently made
partner at Demspey, Cook and Spencer, a prominent law firm
in Denver, Colorado. After a honeymoon in San Diego, the
couple will relocate to Denver."

This better be Maggie's *last* last name. He'd hardly gotten used to her as Eagle Heart. This one was going to be the
hardest for Tom to get used to. Mrs. James Carlson.

Next to the write-up was a picture. The image was a little grainy, but there was Carlson, arm in arm with Maggie.
Rosebud and Nan stood next to Maggie, and Dan and Agnes
were next to Carlson. Everyone looked happy, and the sun
wasn't so bright that they were all squinting.

Tom had to wonder what it all meant. Who would have
guessed that Maggie would ever find someone like Carlson?
Hell, who would have guessed that Carlson would ever find
someone like Maggie? Not him, that was for damn sure.

It had worked out. Low Dog had rolled on the man who
had given him Maggie's name and address in an envelope—
who turned out to be Royce T. Maynard's legal counsel. As-
sault and attempted murder of potential witnesses was the
kind of evidence that couldn't be dismissed on a technical-
ity, and Carlson's replacement had pushed forward with the
case. Maynard was going to be done in by his own hand.
Maybe he'd get to share a cell with Low Dog. Tom could
hope, anyway.

Tom was *happy* for Maggie, he really was. He was even a
little happy for Carlson. But all the joy and smiles and tears
hadn't done a damn thing but remind him of Stephanie. He'd
been happy once. And now that time was over.

"Did you ever think that lousy SOB would up and do something like that?" Hughes chuckled. "I thought you two were buds." The big man was now slapping his knee, as if this was the finest joke in the tristate region. "Betcha he left you off the guest list!"

Tom dropped the newspaper on his desk and leaned back to stare his coworker down. Hughes choked on his chuckle and made the wise decision to find something else to do.

Tom watched Hughes waddle back to his own desk, and then he picked up the paper again. Some investigator, he thought with an inward snort in Hughes's direction. Couldn't even figure that Tom had snapped the shot himself.

Not a bad photo, he decided. If he were a sentimental man, he'd even consider framing the original. After all, those people—Rosebud and Dan, Carlson and now, again, Maggie—were the only people left who cared if he lived or died.

But Tom wasn't a sentimental guy. He dropped the newspaper in the trash.

He had to get back to work.

* * * * *